THE COPPER BULLET

Dr. Bland retires to his office to rest, complaining of a headache. But later, his fellow scientists find him slumped over his desk — dead. In his forehead is a round hole, edged with burn marks. He has apparently shot himself — but there is no sign of a gun. The only clue is a copper bullet, of the type used in a .38 revolver. There is no cartridge cover — indicating that the bullet *has* been fired, and then put there . . .

JOHN RUSSELL FEARN
Edited by PHILIP HARBOTTLE

---◆---

THE
COPPER
BULLET

Complete and Unabridged

LINFORD
Leicester

First published in Great Britain

First Linford Edition
published 2012

British Library CIP Data

Fearn, John Russell, *1908 – 1960.*
 The copper bullet. - -
 (Linford mystery library)
 1. Detective and mystery stories.
 2. Large type books.
 I. Title II. Series
 823.9'12–dc23

 ISBN 978–1–4448–1220–6

Published by
F. A. Thorpe (Publishing)
Anstey, Leicestershire

Set by Words & Graphics Ltd.
Anstey, Leicestershire
Printed and bound in Great Britain by
T. J. International Ltd., Padstow, Cornwall

This book is printed on acid-free paper

1

The Copper Bullet

Dr. Henry Bland, chief of the Atomic Research Centre, was in one of his moods again. Probably overwork. Certainly he looked pale and troubled as he paced up and down the laboratory annex wherein he and two members of the staff were working.

'Death and destruction to millions,' Dr. Bland muttered, coming to a halt and musing. 'That's the thing I can't get over! Here are we in here, working out the complicated equations necessary for nuclear fission and we don't give a thought to the deeper issues.'

'Wouldn't do much good if we did, sir,' remarked the younger of his two colleagues — Jeffrey Travers, research scientist. 'We have experiments to carry out in this pile where we're all imprisoned, so what more is there to be said?'

1

Dr. Bland did not reply. The third man did not speak, either. He was essentially a mathematician, cold-faced and pale-eyed. He did not indulge in the scientific arguments that often brought Bland and young Travers to high words and short tempers.

'I don't mean the possible destruction an atomic mishap here on earth might cause,' Bland said presently, 'though heaven knows that is appalling enough. I'm thinking of the possible effects on *other* universes every time we indulge in atom-splitting! I've thought about it a lot these last few days,' he continued, rubbing his forehead. 'Funny thing, but I think about it most when I get these confounded headaches of mine. Never had one in my life until recently.'

'You surely don't mean,' the third man said incredulously, 'that every time we split atoms we might be destroying other worlds and universes?' He shook his head. 'I know that years ago some unscientific people used to think that the atomic world was simply the microcosm, that the electron was analogous to a planet, that the proton was the central attraction like our own sun — and that the atom itself, the molecular structure, could be likened to a solar system. That we lived in the macrocosm, and — ' he smiled thinly, ' — every time we indulged in atom-splitting we destroyed countless solar systems and maybe millions of living beings, so small that . . . ' he broke off as Bland glared at him.

'Stop talking such damned nonsense, man!' Bland demanded irritably, his thin face working. 'Everybody knows in these days of quantum theory — or they should — that matter as we know it is only a very small portion of our universe, and that if one universe exists, there must be many — perhaps an infinite number of other universes. Our universe is just one component of a vast array of universes, a cosmic mosaic. We've no real idea of what happens at the inter-atomic level, and it's possible that these universes are connected, at the tiny atomic level, through higher dimensional tunnels through spacetime . . . ' he broke off broodingly . . . ' a kind of cosmic umbilical cord. Who's to say that the vast energies released by our atom-splitting experiments might not travel along those cosmic umbilical chords into a neighbouring universe? It is the thought of this merciless destruction which worries me.'

The other scientist frowned thoughtfully. 'I take your point, sir, but what about all the atomic fusion going on in the heart of the sun — and all the other stars in the universe?'

Bland waved a hand dismissively. 'A star is an intensely *dense* concentration of matter — obviously other universes are unlikely to exist within it. I'm taking about here on earth, or in space, where matter is *tenuous* by comparison . . . ' He gave a sigh. 'Anyway, gentlemen, I've talked enough. I'm going to my office for a brief rest. This headache of mine is killing me. And Wilson,' he added to the third man, 'just come along with me, will you? I've some papers to give you.'

The lean-faced mathematician gave a nod and accompanied the professor from the laboratory. Left to himself, Jeffrey Travers reflected for a while on the somewhat peculiar things his superior had said; then with a shrug he returned to his work.

After a while Wilson returned. He seemed as though he were making an effort to control himself even though he did not say anything. He went over to the big locker where he, Travers, and Bland kept some of their equipment and personal belongings, then hurried out again. In a matter of perhaps three minutes he had returned once more.

'The old man wants you, Jeff,' he said. 'Special report, or something.'

Jeff gave a nod and slid from his stool, leaving the laboratory swiftly.

★ ★ ★

Not ten yards from Dr. Bland's private quarters the cleaner was mopping the already immaculate floor that led to the back regions of this heavily guarded atomic-research centre. It was the sound of a gunshot that made him look up abruptly and then around him. Queer noises were numerous in this hive of industry, but there was no mistaking a gun report — and it seemed to have come from the direction of Dr. Bland's sanctum.

The cleaner threw down his mop and began moving swiftly. He arrived in the adjoining corridor just in time to see Wilson gripping Jeffrey Travers tightly. From other doorways down the long, shining length figures in overalls were appearing.

'What on earth's the matter, man?' Wilson was demanding, still holding Jeff tightly. 'What's wrong?'

Jeff pointed back shakily towards Dr. Bland's room.

'He's — he's dead!' he gasped out. 'Shot through the head, I think. I saw him sitting there slumped at his desk and — and I just panicked.'

'You mean he's shot himself?' Wilson demanded blankly.

'I don't know. I just dashed out to get help.'

Wilson looked at the other laboratory employees. 'Get Security right away. I'll take charge for the moment — We'd better go and see what's wrong in Dr. Bland's room.'

He strode into the sanctum, Jeff

following behind him. In silence the other technicians stood looking in. Dr. Bland was in his tubular chair at his antique desk. He had fallen forward so that his head and shoulders sprawled on the blotter. In his high, white forehead was a round hole burned around the edges. That he was stone dead was obvious.

'No sign of a gun,' one of the men said, looking about him.

'No, but — What's that?' Jeff asked, pointing to the antique oak inkstand.

Everybody looked. On the polished woodwork lay a bullet, copper-jacketed, of the type used in a .38 revolver. It had no cartridge cover.

'It looks,' Wilson said slowly, 'as though that bullet has been fired and then put there. The cartridge case should be somewhere around . . . ' He gave a vague glance about him and then added sharply, 'Don't touch anything! Leave that to the experts.'

His order was obeyed and in silence the group stood waiting, wondering, until two officials from the F.B.I., permanently connected on patrol work at the atomic centre, came into the room.

Behind them trooped a surgeon, photographers, and fingerprint experts. When each of these experts had done his job the two F.B.I. men went into action. One asked questions of everybody concerned, including the cleaner; the other examined the room in detail. It was not very long before a .38 revolver was fished out from under the desk at which Bland lay dead.

His finger in the revolver barrel, the official studied the weapon interestedly.

'Why, that's mine!' Jeffrey Travers exclaimed, astonished.

'Oh? Yours?' Cold eyes studied him. 'What's it doing here, Mr. Travers?'

'I just don't know. I usually keep it in my tackle in the annexe. It's licensed. All of us have guns for personal protection since we're on dangerous work.'

'Mmmm.' The official laid the gun on the blotter and removed his finger, then without touching the weapon he sniffed the barrel. 'Recently fired. And this bullet on the inkstand is a thirty-eight. There should be a cartridge somewhere.'

'Right here,' the other man said, and picked it up from beside the bureau . . .

Such was the beginning of things. Almost before he could grasp what was happening Jeff Travers found himself under arrest and committed for trial for the murder of Dr. Bland, bail being refused.

It was during the trial that he realized how hopelessly he was involved. He had been the last man to see Bland alive — for Wilson swore the 'old man' had been fit enough when he had left him for the second time — and it was his gun that had been found. The bullet had been fired from it, ballistics had proved, and the shot had come from short range judging from the burning round the forehead wound. The theory was that the bullet had then been quickly removed and put on the inkstand, though just why Jeff Travers had done this was not very clear.

To the defence's protest that Travers had not had time to do such a thing the prosecution stated that there had been *just* time, and no more. The fact that the hole in Bland's forehead was larger than

9

the bullet itself showed that the hole had been widened to extract the bullet . . .

Added to this was the cleaner's statement about a gunshot — which Jeff Travers himself swore he had never heard — and there was also the known fact that Jeff Travers and Bland had often quarrelled violently over scientific issues.

The inference that the jury could draw was obvious and they came in with a verdict of 'Guilty, with strong recommendations to mercy,' chiefly because the crime had apparently been one of impulse and not pre-meditated.

The way things looked at the end of the trial Jeff Travers was doomed and Grant Wilson was the new head of the Research Centre . . . but one man was not satisfied. Far from it.

The dissatisfied man was the extraordinary Brutus Lloyd. Strictly speaking, this short-statured, bumptious little man was a research chemist, but with degrees in many scientific fields. However, he preferred to study crime to worrying over research problems. So, having a considerable private income with which to indulge his fancy, he had become a holy terror to all criminal organizations. The intolerably conceited Brutus Lloyd was a friend of the city police, always welcome at police headquarters, his scientific know-how having solved many an otherwise inexplicable crime.

That he knew all the details of the Bland affair went without saying. No criminal trial had ever appeared but what he was present throughout the proceedings. The moment he heard the verdict on Jeffrey Travers he left the courtroom, jumped into his car, and drove straight to police headquarters in the city. He was welcomed cordially enough by the bull-necked precinct chief, Inspector Branson. However, Branson's pleasantries began to evaporate before Lloyd's rapier looks.

'Let young Travers be convicted,' Lloyd stated flatly, 'and it will be the biggest miscarriage of justice ever! I never heard of a man being accused on such flimsy evidence!'

'But, Dr. Lloyd, everything fits — '

'Don't argue with me!' Lloyd roared, glaring. 'From the viewpoint of little-minded dolts maybe everything *does* fit in — but not to me. And I am Brutus Lloyd, which makes all the difference. I wish to examine the details again.'

'Can't be done. The trial's over and — '

'You listen to me,' Lloyd broke in deliberately, his eyelids drooping insolently. 'I am going to work on this problem for the scientific interest it possesses. I mean to prove how Bland *really* died, and at the same time give science some information which will knock out its academic eye! As for the trial, it can be cited as a mistrial if new and incontestable evidence should be forthcoming, as it will be with me in charge of things. This demands a brain, not a ninny. Well, what about it?'

Branson swallowed his wrath and went purple in the doing.

'Very well,' he whispered, with strangled patience. 'We can't afford to quarrel with you, Dr. Lloyd: you've helped us too much in the past. Just what do you want exactly?'

'First, all statements by the various people; all photographs, fingerprint reports, and doctor's p.m. statement.'

'I'll have them at your house in an

hour,' Branson promised, and with that Lloyd slammed his untidy derby hat back on his tuft of jet-black hair, and departed.

Branson kept his word and for the remainder of the day Lloyd spent the time in his large house on the city outskirts brooding over the reports. Towards early evening he went out again and back to police headquarters. He caught Inspector Branson just as he was leaving his office.

'I was just going home, Lloyd — '

'I don't care if you're bound for the North Pole. I want you to get some action for me. As the official brain around here — or do I expect too much? — you are the only person with authority.' Lloyd cuffed his battered derby to the back of his head and added, 'Get whatever official permission is needed for us to exhume the body of Bland right away. I want to study his forehead.'

'What the hell for?' Branson sat down heavily and stared. 'And why do you want to examine his forehead?'

'Because the doctor's p.m. report does not satisfy me. I'm not saying he's a liar, mind you, but I do think he has taken too much for granted. I want to verify my conclusions by seeing Bland's body for myself.'

'Well, I suppose I *could* arrange it,' Lloyd admitted. 'Is there anything else in the reports which you find unsatisfactory?'

The sarcasm was not lost upon Lloyd. He gave his ghostly smile for a moment, then lost it and pinned Branson with ice-blue eyes.

'Taken as reports, Branson, they're logical enough — but they ignore many factors. For instance, Professor Bland suffered recently from violent headaches, during which he kept on thinking of the tragedy of destroying other universes every time an atom is split. Did the defence make anything of that? No!'

'Could it?' Branson ventured, mystified.

'Certainly! But it needs talent. A pity. Sometimes, y'know, I am staggered by my own gifts, Branson. However, I think the headaches may answer many things. Then there was the bullet on the inkstand, so conveniently placed. From the photographs it looks to me as though there is a burn on the stand. That right?'

'The stand is right here.' Branson answered, going over to a steel locker. 'It was a court exhibit and now the case is over it has been returned to my custody.' He brought the antique oak stand forward and set it on the desk. To one of the wells a tag was tied, and to the copper bullet which Branson put down on the stand itself.

'Quite intriguing,' Lloyd commented, looking at the stand intently. 'There is a burn on this stand, Branson, approximately four inches long, just under where the bullet is lying. The bullet would not be hot enough to cause it — and anyway it isn't as long as the burn mark. So what did it?'

'Dunno. Cigarette some time, maybe.'

'That long!' Lloyd jumped as though he'd been stung. 'Have a heart, man! I'll make one guess that the burn was caused by something resembling a bullet, but longer and wider, and that the heat was caused by atmospheric friction.'

The Inspector opened his mouth and closed it again. Then he scratched his head. The insolent droop had come back to Lloyd's eyelids.

'You don't follow my reasoning, Branson, do you?'

'Damned if I do!'

'No more than I expected. Few can, which is why I am in a class by myself. However, I've seen all I want to see for the moment, thanks. Now attend to that exhumation for me, will you?'

Branson nodded and turned to the phone, and because Lloyd was Lloyd he got his wish. The body was exhumed that same night, and the following morning, equipped with instruments, Lloyd drove over to the mortuary to make his examination in the presence of deeply puzzled police officials.

It took him three hours, during which time he probed the dead scientist's skull and used portable X-ray apparatus of his own design. This done he drove back to his home with the puzzled but interested Inspector Branson.

'It will certainly surprise you to know, Branson,' Lloyd said, as he and the inspector refreshed themselves with coffee and sandwiches in the comfortable lounge, 'that the projectile which killed Bland came from the inside of his skull to the outside, not from the outside to the in.'

Branson nearly choked over his sandwich and only recovered with a purple face after a few moments. Lloyd regarded this near-apoplexy dispassionately.

'The assumption has been,' Lloyd continued, 'that the bullet was dug out and put on the inkstand. I never believed that, in spite of the prosecution saying Travers had time to do it. He wouldn't anyway: far too risky. My examination of the brain tissue in Bland's skull shows distinctly that something exploded in his head and went outwards through his skull, leaving an apparent bullet mark. The burning was not from close-range fire but from the heat of the projectile itself. You will recall that the hole was too large to match the thirty-eight bullet? That was explained as being because the bullet was dug out. Sheer nonsense! The real reason was that the actual missile of death was both bigger and longer than the thirty-eight bullet.'

'But hang it, Lloyd, the projectile — or whatever it was — *couldn't* come from the inside of Bland's head to the outside! It's against all reason and logic!'

'Don't talk to me about logic!' The eyelids drooped. 'We are dealing here with something extremely scientific — to which Bland himself gave the clue when he spoke of the intra-atomic connections to other universes which are being destroyed by nuclear fission on our part. There is something else, too. The ballistics report says that the bullet on the inkstand was as clean as a dog's tooth, even under an electron microscope.'

'I know. What's wrong with that?'

'What's *wrong* with it?' Lloyd hooted. 'Everything! Sweet nitre, why do I have to deal with such nitwits? A bullet dug out of a brain that quickly, as is assumed, could not be cleaned thoroughly because there wouldn't be time. Traces of tissues would have been bound to adhere to it. Yet none did. Why? Because I don't believe it was ever in Bland's head!'

'I give up,' Branson muttered.

'Naturally! Better men than you have

faltered before my deductions, Branson. However — ' Lloyd got to his feet. 'I have things to do if I'm to clear up this business. I'll tell you what I want you to do whilst I make some preparations in my laboratory. Have young Travers taken to the annexe — which is permitted under police supervision if it may lead to proving his innocence — and have Wilson there too, the new head of the Division. I'll be there around seven o'clock this evening. Get some scientists there also who understand intra-atomic physics and quantum theory. I may need them for verification even though I personally shall not listen to a word they say ... Now I have got to rush. I've a special model to make. See you later.'

Branson nodded in some bewilderment and stared after Lloyd as he hurried energetically from the room.

★   ★   ★

The electric clock in the annex was on the stroke of seven that evening when Lloyd entered. He was travelling light, not even carrying a brief case. He nodded to the assembly and pulled off his battered derby, throwing it down on the nearby table.

Present were Travers, pale and worried; the cold-faced mathematician Wilson; and one or two older men who were recognized experts in the field of atomic science. There was of course Inspector Branson and a couple of plainclothes men keeping guard over Travers.

'Well, gentlemen, all of you are scientists — except our friends of the law,' Lloyd said, digging his hands in his overcoat pockets and looking about him. 'It is because I have happened on something so unique in regard to the late Dr. Bland that I require you scientific gentlemen to verify some of my conclusions. I know I am right because I am rarely anything else, but the public in general may not be entirely satisfied with my word alone . . .

'Now, the law has said that Dr. Bland died from a thirty-eight bullet which was afterwards dug out by Travers. *I* say that Dr. Bland was killed by an intra-atomic projectile, which had travelled from the realm of the infinitely small to the infinitely big!'

There was silence, the men glancing at one another. Wilson tightened his lips and a dawning hope crossed Travers' young face.

'Whatever killed Dr. Bland came from inside his head,' Lloyd continued dogmatically. 'That fact is now beyond cavil. I have every medical angle to support the theory. Such a thing could not happen unless it came from some other dimension or some other space. Quantum theory postulates that our universe is only one of a myriad of other universes. There is no reason why some of those universes might not contain living beings, existing in another dimension. To us, it could have been microscopic in size, in just the same way it is possible that we, in our apparently great universe — though size is relative — are actually a mere speck in the make-up of some titanic creature who inhabits a greater universe — outside *us*.'

Lloyd sat down and began to emphasise with an acid-stained hand.

'If super-beings outside our universe began to shatter our planetary system by what, to them, would be nuclear fission, we might feel like getting our own back. Were we clever enough we could do it by expanding our size, by travelling in an ever-growing machine which finally would burst through the known universe into a higher dimension, and into a mightier one beyond. That I believe is what happened in this case! From somewhere in the infinite Small intelligent beings set off in a machine to cross atomic space, maybe to find the cause of the constant nuclear explosions occurring in their universe. It is possible they were clever enough to know, by receiving thought waves, that Dr. Bland was at the head of the concern, and so their ever-growing machine was directed into the atomic spaces within his very brain!

'He complained of violent headaches, set up no doubt by the ever-increasing pressure of the enlarging machine. It at last burst its own space and came into ours, an object slightly bigger than a bullet, a perfectly made but extremely tiny object like a space machine, carrying beings maybe a quarter of a centimetre high. It passed through Bland's skull and settled on the inkstand, which would appear to those within the machine to resemble a plain. The heat of the energy change and brief atmospheric friction made it hot enough to burn the wood of the inkstand. I also believe that these beings had the power of thought-transference, and because of their thoughts Bland knew in advance what was coming, but he could only interpret it as horror at the prospect of destroying — and having destroyed — so many other universes.'

'This is ridiculous!' Wilson protested. 'What about the bullet?'

'It is *not* ridiculous!' Lloyd declared. 'For here is the atom-ship itself . . . ' And from his overcoat pocket he took a gleaming copper object like a cigar. It had small, perfectly made portholes and a conning tower.

'Why, that's mine!' Wilson exclaimed in amazement. 'Where did you find it — ?'

He stopped, confused, and looked about him. In amazement every eye was fixed upon him. He hesitated for a moment and then swung to a steel locker. Unfastening it swiftly he searched within and brought a second copper cylinder to view, not unlike the one Lloyd possessed. He swung round sharply, to meet a levelled gun in Lloyd's hand.

'As a private citizen, Mr. Wilson, I can use a gun to keep you covered whereas the police cannot,' he explained. With his free hand he tossed down his copper model on the bench.

'Model work is but another of my gifts,' he explained. 'As I imagined an atomic space machine would look. I'm glad you tripped yourself up, Mr. Wilson. I'll take that.'

He seized the copper cylinder from Wilson's hand and set it carefully on the bench. Wilson breathed hard.

'All right, so you tripped me,' he admitted. 'I didn't murder anybody, though, so you can't hold that against me.'

'No, but you did your best to get Travers convicted! Why?'

'Because he is a nuclear physicist and I

am just a mathematician. The Board would have elected him as chief of this unit over me after Bland's death, so I got him out of the way. There was a second reason. I wanted that atom ship for myself. I had intended to examine it thoroughly and open a branch of atomic science — atom travelling — which would have made me world famous.'

'Evidently you have a mathematician's agile brain, Wilson,' Lloyd commented. 'From the reports of your actions I will outline what happened — and don't anybody dare interrupt me! You went with Dr. Bland to his sanctum as he asked. When there you saw him die, saw the projectile land on the inkstand. You are scientist enough to realize what had happened. You thought fast. Here was a new departure in science — atom travel — performed by beings from an unknown dimension. It could mean great power for you if you kept the secret. You returned here, took Travers' gun from the locker, and went back to the sanctum. You fired a bullet silently somehow, probably by the old trick of smothering it in a cushion,

25

which you afterwards hid. The bullet you put on the inkstand and took away the cooled atom-ship. The revolver you threw under the desk. It had no fingerprints. You must have put your own on it when firing it but naturally wiped them off again — and any of Travers' also.

'Next you told Travers that Bland wanted him. He obeyed. You created a sound like a gunshot in the corridor where it could be heard — possibly by bursting a paper bag or something. The rest was simple. Travers had no alibi: it was known he did not like Bland, and there the thing was. How I arrived at my theory of an atom-ship I have already explained to Inspector Branson — Well, Wilson how right am I?'

'Dead right,' the mathematician growled. 'I'd forgotten such scientific detectives as you even existed. But I did not *kill* anybody and I still claim that that atom-ship is mine.'

'Not yours exclusively,' Lloyd replied. 'It is the property of science as a whole — a revelation of life within the infinite Small. As for you, my friend, your efforts to get Travers accused of murder are for the law to deal with.'

Lloyd turned away and looked at the perfect machine on the bench. With a small pair of tweezers he opened the airlock — with which Wilson had obviously already tampered — and rolled the ship on its side. Queerly dressed but perfectly formed creatures, no larger than a match-head, rolled out. They were stiff in death.

'A pity,' Lloyd sighed. 'The journey killed them, otherwise — with my genius and theirs — what a story there would have been to tell!'

2

Black Saturday

The individual experiences of many thousands of people on that 'Black Saturday', as it has since become known, have been retailed throughout the world. But there is one random experience, that of Robert Maitland and Irene Carr, which has not yet been recorded. In many ways it is typical of millions, and is therefore undistinguished. It is, however, notable in that these two ordinary people, caught in circumstances very similar to millions of others and equally mystified by them, were yet able to deduce for themselves the simple explanation of what had occurred — the explanation that eluded most of us until the scientists, with all the data they needed, presented it to the wondering world.

Think back. Recall your own bafflement, your sense of utter helplessness, your *fear*, and you may grant the noteworthiness of this particular experience of two people who were no better equipped than millions of their kind to realize the nature of the apparent catastrophe which had overtaken them. Yet, amid all the acclamation we have accorded the scientists, we have entirely overlooked the perseverance and good sense of those few who, like these two, refused to give way to despair until they had tried to work out the problem for themselves.

Dr. Robert Maitland lived, at that time, in a modest house in Windermere. His practice was small but full of promise: he was making a name for himself among the villagers and the rustic community of the Lake District. On the morning of July 8th he was awakened early by a telephone call. One of his patients, badly injured in a farming accident the day before, had taken a turn for the worse. In the chill of the summer dawn, Maitland listened to the high, tremulous voice of the stricken man's wife over the wire. He promised to be over right away, rubbed the sleep out of his eyes, and set about dressing hastily.

Robert Maitland was not the type that is addicted to nervous fancies. He stood five feet ten, was solidly built, and his lean, swarthy face had strength and responsibility in every line. And yet — he was seeing things. Things that, in the urgency of his dressing and with the purpose of his errand uppermost in his thoughts, did not immediately absorb his attention, yet which vaguely puzzled him.

For instance, as he brushed his thick, dark hair hurriedly before the mirror, he could have sworn that his reflection moved very slightly from side to side. A measure might have shown at least an inch of movement, as if he were swaying on his feet, though he was certain he was standing perfectly still. Then, through his bedroom window, he could see across the rolling pastureland to the distant mountains grouped about Helvellyn; and as he looked it seemed that the mountains glided slowly sideways, then drifted back into their normal position.

There were no warps in the window glass; he was sure of that. The mirror, too, was a good one. Maitland closed his eyes

30

tightly, opened them again, and decided that he felt well enough. It must be some slight liverishness, or perhaps it was just tiredness — he wasn't as completely awake yet as he'd thought. It would soon pass . . .

He was, of course, unaware that millions of people all over the world were trying to account for similar manifestations at that precise moment. Nor did he realize that the world's scientists were even then busily communicating among themselves, seeking some clue to the peculiar phenomena they had observed.

Maitland left the house after scribbling a note to his housekeeper that he had gone on an urgent call. He hurried outside to the garage. It was getting warmer now. The sun was struggling through the fast dispersing mists from the valleys and there was every sign that the day would be a perfect one. Then, on his way down the narrow drive leading to the garage, Maitland paused and rubbed his forehead as he stared bewildered before him.

The garage building straight ahead, with its bright green doors, was moving

31

over to the right — soundlessly. The fence alongside it was moving, too! This time there was no mistake about it. The garage shifted at least two feet and came to a halt. At the same time the gravel drive *bent* suddenly, at a spot immediately in front of Maitland, so that he had to take a distinct, sharp corner to continue towards the garage doors.

Uncertain, he went forward slowly, turning sharply to the right even though he knew it was an idiotic thing to do. How foolish it was he discovered when he felt himself stumbling over the edge of the drive on to the flower bed at the side — yet apparently he was still on the gravel pathway. Abruptly he realized that he was faced with the impossible. He seemed to be treading on something he could see only two feet away from him, yet he couldn't *feel* the thing his eyes told him he *was* treading on. Then, even as he wrestled silently with the riddle, the garage and the drive moved back without a sound into their accustomed position — and Maitland stared open-mouthed, conscious of the fact that he was actually standing in the soil of the flower bed two feet away from the drive.

Delusions? Incipient insanity? He considered both possibilities with a cold, professional detachment, but neither seemed to fit. This was something new, vitally different — and as yet beyond explanation. He stepped back gingerly on to the drive, found it solid enough, and went on to open the garage doors. To his relief, everything remained apparently normal as he backed the car out. He left it with the engine ticking over as he closed the doors. Then he clambered back into the driving seat and swerved out on to the road.

To the home of his patient was some twenty miles' journey along valley roads, between lofty hills and through quaint old villages. He drove swiftly, but not so swiftly that he could not admire the beauty of the countryside as he went. The sun now was high above the hills, blazing down with gathering heat, picturing itself in a myriad microscopic reflections from the dew-soaked grass and flowers bordering the road. As he drove on, Maitland forgot his strange visual aberration

— until he was cruelly reminded of it.

He had climbed out of the depths of the valley where his home lay. To his right were towering hills with scrubby fields nestling at their bases; to his left was a smooth panorama stretching for fifteen miles across pastureland, tarns, and lush valley sides. Such was the aspect when the narrow road he was traversing bent suddenly, directly ahead of him — not normally, but as he approached it. Simultaneously, the grass bank at the side of the road shifted to accommodate the bend.

Maitland put on the brakes and came to a stop. He knew perfectly well that this road did *not* bend ahead of him: it went straight on towards Wilmington village. The only curve in it at all was a slight one about half a mile further on, where stood a lonely telephone box. If he went round this pseudo-curve now, he might run over the edge of the road and down the grass slope. No sense in risking that.

'Something's up!' he muttered, convinced at last that it was not his eyes nor his health that was at fault, but that something in the nature of a mirage — or a series of them — must have occurred in this locality; though what could have caused such a thing was beyond him. Finally, he got out of the car with the intention of studying this particular mirage more closely. But he took only three strides forward before he stopped, tottering dizzily in the middle of the road.

In that moment he was frightened, really scared, as he had never been before. For all of a sudden everything about him seemed to have gone completely crazy. The whole landscape as far as he could see was shifting violently. The fifteen-mile stretch of country before him was sweeping sideways at diabolical speed — shearing off to the west as a towering wall of blackness appeared to race in from the east, moving everything before it!

Maitland just stood and stared, petrified. There was no sound as the amazing thing occurred; only the titanic shadow which raced towards him with the speed of a total eclipse. Within a few seconds it passed over him, and the bent road ahead was blotted from sight. He stood, now, drenched in darkness, feeling no other sensation but a supreme dread.

It was several seconds before he could recover himself sufficiently to move, and then he began to retrace his steps slowly and cautiously towards the car, hands outstretched gropingly before him. Not a thing was visible — except the sun, shining high in a sky still strangely blue! Shining, yet failing to light anything . . .

Feeling his way forward, he came up against the bonnet of the car and clung to it gratefully. He couldn't see even the dimmest outline of the car itself.

He stood and gazed up at the sun, thankful that it, at least, held to normalcy but this relief was soon denied. One moment it was there in the dark blue sky; the next, it had started to sink towards the western horizon with incredible speed. It dropped like a meteor, vanished in the all-enveloping blackness that formed the limits of the landscape, and was gone.

Now it was utterly dark. Dreadfully, horribly dark . . .

★   ★   ★

There was something wrong out there in the depths of space; something so incredibly strange that the scientists who tried to examine the mystery found their accumulated centuries of knowledge faltering. It had begun with the amazing antics of the stars neighbouring on the Milky Way. Fixed apparently for eternities of time in their courses, arranged much as the ancients had seen them when they stared up at them uncomprehending, they had now completely changed position — and in some cases disappeared entirely. Sagittarius, Hercules, Antares, Cepheus — they were visibly shifting across the wastes of heaven, moving at such an unthinkable velocity that the minds of the watching astronomers reeled, used though they were to cosmic speeds. And the Milky Way itself was shifting, bearing towards the westernmost limb of the sky.

The amazing part of the phenomenon, apart from its very occurrence, was the suddenness with which it had developed. On the night of July 7th the world's observatories had noticed nothing unusual. But on the 8th, between the hours of midnight and dawn, these fantastic perambulations of the stars were only too evident. Though it just couldn't be, because it shattered every basic law of astronomy. Yet it *was* . . . And from the space which the stars had deserted gleamed new and unknown constellations, hosts of heaven that made complete chaos of the world's star-maps. The astronomers immediately got in touch with one another and discussed the problem. All had to admit themselves baffled. But, hesitating to make the same admission to their respective governments, they agreed to make no announcement of their startling observations until they had been able to study the phenomenon further and consider the enigma in the light of additional data. Given time, they agreed, they might find something to account for it. And that is where they made their great mistake.

Earth, in her majestic million-miles-a-minute sweep through the universe, was moving irresistibly towards that part of the heavens whose aspects had changed so mysteriously. And, although at that time the fact could not be detected, the disturbance — the Fault — was also moving towards Earth at a similar speed. So the whole of Earth's peoples had been caught unaware by the Fault.

★ ★ ★

The human mind, psychologists tell us, can absorb the most violent of shocks and still function. But it was a long time before Maitland found he could think intelligently, without letting blind panic scatter his half-formed thoughts. As he struggled to banish his primitive fears he searched the blackness around him, still clinging to the car bonnet, his only link with reality.

Here on the ground the darkness was absolute, and he could not discern the slightest hint of anything. But up in the sky from which the sun had streaked, minutes before, there were now myriads of stars! To Maitland, who had no precise astronomical knowledge, these stars looked normal enough; but an expert would have noticed at once that not many of them were familiar and that the few recognizable constellations were far away from their customary positions.

Night, when it should be 9 a.m.? A sun that disappeared from the sky in a flash? This was a problem beyond all understanding. Yet Maitland knew the elementary fact that the sudden shifting of such a vast body as the sun should cause cataclysmic disturbances, perhaps throw Earth right out of its orbit. And yet everything was quite steady, without even the suggestion of a tremor. This point resolved, he felt a little better. He was still alive, with his feet on solid ground. But he was submerged in the inexplicable —

He stopped suddenly, listening. There were sounds ahead of him. Uneasy feet shambling over the gravel of the road.

'Hello there!' he called.

'Hello!' It was a girl's voice that answered. It was shaken, yet somehow filled with unquenchable courage.

'I'm here.' Maitland shouted. 'Come towards my voice.'

The halting steps advanced again, but nothing came out of the darkness. That was the queer thing. Though there were stars overhead, Earth lay in an abyss from which every spark of light had gone. Maitland groped with both hands as the footsteps came nearer.

'Thank heaven I've — found somebody,' the girl faltered, close by his ear. 'I was just wondering what to do. What's — what's *happened*?'

'You're asking me!' he laughed. 'I'm as bewildered — and probably as scared — as you. I — er — I'm Dr. Maitland, of Windermere,' he said as the girl's outstretched hand gripped his arm.

'I'm Irene Carr.' They clasped hands in the darkness. 'This is the last day of my holiday — Last Day, indeed! I was on a hike to Rydal Water when — it — happened. The — the sun's gone out, hasn't it? That's what it must mean! I know scientists have said something like this would happen one day.'

'Yes, but not like this!' Maitland protested. 'That must be a slow process, over millions of years. This is something different — and quite sudden! We had no warning . . . '

They were silent, oppressed by the unfathomable. Maitland found himself collected enough now, to wonder with intense curiosity what the girl looked like. He was intrigued by her voice: it was slow and mellow with a slight Midlands accent, and he knew instinctively that she was young and possibly attractive. If only he could *see*.

'I know!' he said suddenly, and felt in his pocket for his cigarette lighter. He flicked it, but the flint made no sparks. Then he gave a yelp as, in feeling round the wick, he burned his fingers in invisible flame.

'It *is* working, then?' Irene Carr whispered in wonder, when he explained what had happened. 'Yet we can't see it . . . Do you suppose we've — gone blind?'

'With the stars visible up there?'

'I hadn't noticed — ' She gave a little gasp of surprise. 'Yes, there are stars — billions of them. But no sun — '

'And yet . . . ' Maitland drew a deep breath and considered. 'And yet,' he went on, awed, 'I can feel the sun's heat on the back of my neck. Just as though it's still there.'

The girl was silent as she evidently checked up on his extraordinary finding.

He didn't know whether to believe it himself until she said simply:

'You're right. There *is* heat. I can feel it, too, on the backs of my hands. Yet there's no sun!'

It struck Maitland what an impossible conversation they were keeping up. At the back of his mind, too, was the remembrance of a man who lay on a bed in the dark some ten miles away.

'I wonder if I can drive the car?' he said abruptly. 'Let's see what we can do. There *is* a car here, you know!' He thumped the bonnet with his fist.

'I'll take your word for it,' the girl answered, still trying to sound calm.

Maitland took her arm and they moved cautiously together over the rough surface of the roadway, felt their way round to the car door and clambered inside. Here, with the roof of the car shutting out the stars above, the darkness was crushing; it wasn't even possible to see the outlines of the windows. But by stooping they could see part of the starry sky through the glass, and Maitland thought he caught a brief glimpse of the girl's head silhouetted against the stars, though the outline was blurred and unreal. He pressed the self-starter, and the engine throbbed immediately — a good, wholesome sound in a world that no longer made sense. Then he switched on the headlamp, but not the remotest suggestion of light appeared.

'No good.' He switched off. 'Can't drive in this.'

They both sat in silence for a while, listening to each other's breathing.

'You know,' the girl said presently, 'it's funny. I've read stories where this sort of thing happens, and everything turns out all right. But when it happens to *you*, when everything you've known and trusted lets you down and leaves you blind and bewildered, you just don't know what to do. I suppose,' she went on musingly, her voice steadier as she got to grips with the problem, 'that there *is* an answer?'

'A scientist might have one,' Maitland suggested. 'I'm not a scientist; I'm a doctor.'

'I'm a school teacher . . . But, look, we've both got a fair degree of intelligence. We can reason this thing out, can't we?'

Maitland didn't answer. Thoughts were hurrying through his mind. Memory was at work, piecing together the incredible events of the morning. The mirror reflection that trembled; the garage that shifted position; the landscape that had been swept sideways by an advancing wall of darkness . . .

'All right, Miss Carr. We — '

'I'd rather you called me Irene. After all, we're in this together.'

'Irene it is, then — and mine's Bob. As you say, here we are, two people without any specialized knowledge, but familiar with rudimentary facts. You will be especially, as a teacher. Now, if the sun had really plunged into the deeper universe as it appeared to do, the Earth and all neighbouring planets would have been wiped out in the terrific gravitational change. But that hasn't happened. We are quite safe and undisturbed; the world still moves in its proper orbit. And that means that the sun's dive into obscurity was a — a delusion.'

'Yes,' the girl said, pondering. 'Yes, that's right.'

'On top of that,' he went on, 'we can feel the heat of the sun just as if it were still there. In fact, in this car it is getting uncomfortably warm, and only sunshine — or, rather, heat — can explain it. That shows that the sun *is* still there, although we cannot see it. If it were something that had destroyed the sun utterly, its light *and* heat would be gone and the Earth would grow cold as its stored warmth leaked out into space. That, again, is not happening. It is night, but as hot as any July day should be.'

'And down here, on the Earth's surface,' Irene supplemented, 'no light whatever will function. And the sun went out of sight *after* light failed down here.'

They considered this aspect of the problem for a while in silence. Then Maitland spoke again, his voice vibrant with discovery.

'Doesn't that seem to suggest something which first involved the Earth, and the sun afterwards? Supposing that idea is right: what can we deduce from it? We know that what will bend visible light will not bend heat. Remember the old college experiment? A prism of glass will bend light out of its normally straight path, but that same prism is opaque to heat, involving a totally different set of circumstances. To refract heat waves we would use a prism of rock salt, or something like that.'

'Refraction,' the girl repeated slowly. Her voice sharpened. 'Refraction! Dr. Maitland — Bob — do you think that could be the answer? You know, like a spoon in a tumbler of water? It looks sharply bent, but really it's not. Or like a mirage, which makes things appear miles away from where they really are!'

'A mirage — on a colossal scale — Yes, I'd thought of something like that.' Maitland began a meticulous searching of his mind, trying to remember all he had learned about light. 'We know that we see objects because of the light emitted or reflected from them. Then, if by some fluke the light waves no longer traveled in straight lines, we would not see the object at which we looked.'

'Right!' the girl agreed. 'I know a few things about light, too. I've taught it in physics class. The first law of refraction is that the incident ray — the normal, straight one, that is — and the refracted ray both lie in one plane; and the second law is that a ray of light passing obliquely from a less dense to a more dense medium is bent towards the perpendicular at the point of incidence. Good heavens!' she went on rapidly. 'It's beginning to make sense. Before this happened did it seem to you that things kept jumping out of place and back again?'

'No doubt of it,' Maitland declared, rather overcome by her growing control of the situation.

'Then doesn't it suggest that the Earth has come into contact with something — some region of space — that is a denser medium than usual, and because of it all light waves are bent to one side? Something so enormous in extent that it involves the sun and, maybe, the whole solar system? So, light waves don't move straight any more, but heat waves remain unaffected.'

★　★　★

A scientist might have been very proud — or very jealous — of Irene Carr at that moment. Without any special qualifications, reasoning out the problem solely from elementary principles derived from her school-teaching, she had arrived at the amazing solution. Refraction — a gigantic mirage! This was the theory that was being discussed at that very moment by scientists all over the world, by long distance telephone and radio. Light alone was affected: that was the cardinal point. Every other kind of radiation was normal.

Something, somehow, was bending the light waves out of the straight line.

'But — but the stars!' Maitland exclaimed. 'We can see them perfectly!'

They lowered the car windows and looked outside. The darkness was so intense that it made their eyes ache. It was a relief to gaze up to where the sky was still dusted with the multi-millions of stars that had sprung into being at the start of the mystery. Maitland and the girl were quiet for a long time, two puny mortals grappling with an infinite problem in a lightless world. Then Irene spoke again.

'Where,' she asked, 'is the Milky Way? My astronomy isn't so good, but I do know that smudgy band like curdled milk. And it just isn't there anymore.'

She was right. That swirling galaxy from which the Earth itself had been born was not visible. Neither, if it came to that, were Sirius, Procyon, Pollux or Betelgeuse, though neither she nor Maitland knew enough to be aware of it. And the Pole Star, famous since time began —

'No Pole Star!' Maitland said, astounded.

Impressed by this new discovery, they clambered out of the car and stood holding on to it as though it were their last material support in a world doomed to everlasting dark. Soft wind, warm and summery, stirred the invisible grass at the side of the road.

'Do you suppose,' Irene said, stumbling round to where Maitland was standing, 'that the thing which is warping light waves is causing us to see stars which ordinarily we wouldn't see? That mirage again?'

'You mean stars beyond our normal range of vision?'

'Yes. Why not? Space is a big place. There are countless trillions of stars we never see in the ordinary way. But if the light from them were bent enormously out of focus we would see them — are seeing them now. By the same token, at some distant point from Earth our sun is probably visible — and the Milky Way. Maybe the inhabitants of an unknown world are wondering at this moment how the unknown sun and galaxy got into their sky and where *their* usual stars have gone!'

'Yes,' Maitland whispered. 'By heaven — yes! A huge light-wave warp, bending everything light-years out of its usual track. I don't know how you worked it out, but it's the only possible explanation. It just *has* to be right!'

'After all,' she went on, more confidently, 'refraction has no definite limits: a mirage can take place within a few feet of the observer or cover dozens of miles. In this case, light waves may be bent millions of miles out of — ' She gave a little gasp as a new thought struck her. 'Of course! Remember how the sun appeared to streak towards the west, and then disappeared? That must have been when the thing came between us and the sun. It wasn't the sun itself that skidded sideways; it was his lightwaves. He's still there!' She stared blindly upwards.

'At least,' Maitland said uneasily, 'we won't freeze! But this is all so impossible — a world where no light will operate. I wonder what's going on in the cities — out on the oceans — in the air? I never stopped to think about it until now.'

Neither of them dared to voice the thoughts that were in both their minds. In any case, the rest of the world was far away, remote. Maitland reached out and caught the girl's arm.

'Let's sit on the grass bank. Too oppressive in the car . . . '

Holding on to each other, they scuffed their feet over the gravel to the side of the lane, groped for the grassy bank and settled down on it, staring into the black void. They gazed anew at the unfamiliar stars that gave no light down here, because once their light waves reached an object they had become so completely refracted that it was not visible at all. Every object on the surface of the Earth was affected in the same way. The area of refraction was so vast that any image-reflection veered right off the Earth itself into surrounding space. It was quiet, too. Only the wind out of the blackness, gentle, caressing, like a comforting hand in deepest sorrow. No birds, no sounds of country life. No friendly voices of other human beings . . .

'Suppose,' Irene whispered, 'it goes on — and on?'

It was the human being in her that was speaking now. Cold logic had given way before natural emotion — before fear.

'It will be the end, I suppose' Maitland said soberly. 'The end of the world. Without the sun, Man couldn't survive.

'But we've *got* the sun,' she insisted. 'It's there — warming us. It's the absence of light that's the problem. If we could only get over that — We might, underground. Maybe this thing the Earth has run into won't act below the surface. We might live down there, like — like Morlocks.'

'If it goes on,' Maitland said slowly, 'it'll mean the end of vegetation as we know it; the end of staple crops, of everything that relies on photosynthesis. A new species of fungoid plants might come into being — '

'And yet, on the surface, we'll still get sunburned, because the ultra-violet rays are unaffected.'

The whole crazy paradox quenched their conversation then. Though neither of them would admit it, even to themselves, deep down inside of them they felt a grim fear. The inborn instinct of the primitive, handed down through unguessable ages, was not to be set aside without a struggle. Darkness was ever to be dreaded . . .

'It's odd, in the midst of this,' Maitland said at length, 'but I keep wondering what you look like.'

The girl's laugh sounded soft and ghostly in the blackness. 'If this ever goes, you'll see,' she murmured. 'But you might be disappointed.'

Maitland smiled bitterly to himself. If this goes — ! She was fearing, even as he was, that it might never go. Earth had, perhaps, plunged forever into an area of refraction where all light was dead.

'Wish I knew the time,' he growled, raising his wristwatch and staring into the blackness. Then an idea struck him. He felt for his penknife and, after a moment's fumbling prized open the watch and felt gently for the hands.

'Ten to twelve.' He whistled. 'Nearly noon. Who'd imagine it?'

'Where were you going when this happened?' the girl inquired.

'I was going to see a patient . . . Look, there's a telephone box about half a mile down the road. I think I ought to try and reach it and give his wife a ring. This might go on all day. Do you want to stay here or — '

'Not likely!'

She grasped his hand and he helped her to her feet. Linking arms, they began to walk unsteadily down the lane, feeling before them at every yard. It was hard going, and they could not immediately rid themselves of the impression that they had been suddenly blinded in a world that was normal for everyone but themselves. Instinctively they kept listening for onrushing cars, until gradually they realized how unnecessary it was. Everything was blotted out completely, just as they were. For once Nature had the complete upper hand of her erring, quarrelsome children.

'Half a mile,' Irene said as they shuffled along. 'That's a long way, in this. How will you know when we get there?'

'It's just in a slight bend of the road. We'll do our best, anyway. It's better than sitting still waiting and wondering how it's all going to end. Sooner or later we should get to Wilmington village. We'll need food — I haven't had my breakfast yet!'

'And I've nothing with me,' the girl sighed. 'I was planning to eat at roadhouses on the way . . . Well, let's hope it will pass soon.'

★ ★ ★

In truth, nobody knew when it would pass; not even the scientists who were engrossed in the phenomenon. In totally dark observatories the world over, they were still discussing it with each other across land and sea, exchanging reports and impressions. Caught unawares by the terrific speed with which the Fault had developed, they had had no time to estimate its area. It might be untold light-centuries in extent, in which case Earth would not swim clear of it for hundreds of years. If, on the other hand, it was a mere patch as cosmic distances are reckoned, it would soon be left behind.

On one thing they were all agreed: something in space — they freely admitted they did not know what — was altering the incident rays of light so tremendously that laws presumed immutable had been completely revoked. The *something* must be a medium that was transparent to heat yet highly refractive to light; perhaps a semi-gaseous envelope, non-poisonous, created in the first instance by the explosion of a long extinct sun. This theory was extended tentatively, and for the time being it had to suffice. To a race that does not yet know exactly what space is, there is no shame in not understanding the real nature of the Fault. It may be centuries before we shall know the truth . . .

'I think,' Maitland said, 'the phone box is just a few yards further on, to our left.

He and the girl had come to the slight bend in the road: they could sense it with their feet as they advanced. Carefully they edged their way along, groping in the dark as they went. For a while they encountered the wire fence at the side of the road. Then suddenly they blundered into hard glass and steel.

'It's it!' cried Irene.

Maitland tugged the door open, groped for the instrument and lifted the receiver. He was thankful that this rural district still did not use the dialling system. Wondering if he would get a reply, he put the receiver to his ear.

'Hello!' came a girl's voice, quite composed.

'Er — can you get me Wilmington Seven Nine?' Maitland asked.

'I'll try, sir. I suppose you can't tell me your number?'

'Impossible. I'm in total darkness. How is it where you are?'

58

'Well, they tell me it's blacker than midnight,' the girl answered. 'I wouldn't know, though. I'm blinded, and trained as a telephone operator. They've called me out on emergency duty . . . Wilmington Seven Nine. Just a moment — ' Then: 'Insert money, please!'

Maitland fumbled with coins. There was the friendly buzzing of the ringing tone as he waited in the darkness. He could hear Irene Carr breathing gently beside him as she stood wedged invisibly between door and frame.

'Hello!' came a thin voice in the receiver.

'That Mrs. Andrews?' he asked quickly. 'Dr. Maitland speaking.'

'Oh, thank God to hear another voice, doctor!' cried the woman, fervently. 'What in heaven's name has happened to the world? Is — is it the Judgment Day at last?'

'I wouldn't know, Mrs. Andrews — but I agree it's pretty ghastly. I'd like to know how your husband is. I'm stranded some ten miles from your place — '

'You don't need to rush yourself, doctor.' The voice was strangely calm, now. 'Something's happened to my husband that I don't rightly understand. When everything went dark he just lay abed and said something about he knew God was everywhere. Then he said he'd never thought about God while life went by, day after day, like clockwork. But now everything's still and dark and quiet, he says he can feel God near him. That's the truth, doctor. And he's goin' to be all right, I'm sure of it! He's sleeping quite peaceful, now.'

'That's fine,' Maitland said. 'I'll come and look at him the moment the darkness passes.'

He put the telephone back, brushed Irene's shoulder as he grasped the door. She stepped out into the road, and they stood side by side in the stygian gloom.

'Everything all right?' she inquired.

He told her what Mrs. Andrews had said. 'He seems to have made a remarkable recovery — at least for the present. I'll have to see him when I can.'

'I think I can understand it,' she mused. 'Normally, when we're healthy and active, we're inclined to take a lot for granted, just as we took the smooth working of the universe for granted — until now. It's only at times like these, when everything goes out of gear that we have to stop and think about such things. And when we find ourselves out of our depth, unable to make sense of what has happened, there's nothing left to lean on but the Almighty.'

Maitland remained silent, holding Irene's arm. Sensing her nearness, he found himself longing more than ever to see what kind of girl this was who had such a simple solution for everything that baffled him. He turned aside and, just for a moment, he fancied he *could* see her. There was the faintest suggestion of a rounded chin, a straight nose, dimly outlined against the blackness beyond. Yes, and a slender figure . . .

While he stared disbelievingly, the silhouette took on depth. He saw the glint of light creep into hair of copper brown; and then she came out of the abyss like a vision, staring back at him with wide blue eyes that began to narrow beneath the impact of returning sunshine. Around her the landscape came gradually into view, as though floodlights were being turned on, slowly —

'Great God!' he whispered, and jerked his gaze upward. Then they both fell back, hands over their faces, as the stars paled out of the sky before an advancing tide of ever-deepening grey. Grey which merged into white, into blue. Then, blinding in its intensity, the sun rose suddenly from the west where it had disappeared, and came to a stop at the zenith.

It was high noon. The Earth had swept clear of the Fault.

3

Death came Flying

The smooth-nosed, black squad car purred its way along the lamp-lit esplanade, carefully threading past groups of raucous, paper-hatted holidaymakers until the pressure of the crowd brought the car to a stop on the fringes of the Longbeach Pleasure Fair.

Plainclothes Inspector Grew dismounted from the car, sniffed the warm, off-sea breeze, which was fragrant also with the various odours of petrol, paraffin and fish-and-chips, and signalled to the two uniformed sergeants inside the car to accompany him. Why he'd been called out on a Bank Holiday evening to investigate an accident was more than he knew. He figured on handing over the job to the squad men as soon as possible and getting back to that game of chess with his new son-in-law.

It was but 10 p.m., and the booths and

sideshows were still active. The air was a veritable cacophony of harsh recorded music, steam organs blaring to make themselves heard above the crashing of dodgem cars and the roar of the giant racer and its small brother switchbacks. Out of the whole noisy whirl of contraptions, one huge machine — the chair-o-plane — stood silent and arc-lit, its score of dangling seats swinging gently like the glass prisms from a chandelier. Inspector Grew frowned and winced as the crash of firing from a rifle-range went off almost at his elbow and he motioned his colleagues towards the silent machine. If there was one place on this earth he disliked visiting, it was a tinsel and sawdust 'paradise' such as this. Only God knew, he reckoned, why people wasted time and good money here. He'd be glad when the holiday season was over. The town would become peaceful and 'livable-in' again.

A nondescript-looking youth with tow hair and a cigarette drooping from his lips eyed them sullenly as the three men mounted the raised circular platform that should have been revolving at high speed.

'Where's the trouble here?'

The youth glared at Grew, then flicked away his cigarette stub. 'Out back here. I'll take you,' he snapped.

Grew followed him off the chair-o-plane machine through a fringe of hoop-la and other stalls into the comparative backwater of the parking ground, where, away from the glare and almost silent except for the pounding of three or four steam traction engines that supplied power and light to the amusement park, motor-caravans and tents were clustered about to form the living quarters of the show people. The youth paused outside a small square marquee, glowing like a lampshade in the darkness.

'In there.'

Grew frowned at the tow-head's obvious incivility, then put out a hand to the flap door of the marquee, and entered, followed by Sergeants Watson and Dooley.

A spruce, professional-looking man in tweeds rose immediately from beside a camp bed along one side of the marquee. Grew recognised him as Duncan, one of the town's foremost medical men. The camp bed was ominously burdened with a white-sheeted form, and there were two other people present, a check-suited, cigar-smoking man and blonde woman of apparently forty or so. She was flashily dressed in black satin, and the smoke from her cigarette curled from fingertips blood-red with nail varnish. She and the man — sitting on plain wooden chairs in front of a baize-topped card table — looked up as the Doctor greeted Inspector Grew.

'Hello Grew, old man. Sorry to spoil your evening and all that — but — well, mine's spoilt too,' he added in an undertone nodding towards the camp bed. 'Shocking job here.'

Grew walked with him to the camp bed and raised a corner of the white sheet, then after some moments let it drop. 'Station sergeant said something about an accident on the chair-o-plane. What happened?'

The doctor hesitated a moment. 'Apparently,' he said after a while. 'The chap was drunk. Forgot to fasten the safety chain and was flung out as the machine reached full speed. Hit one of the concrete pillars supporting the giant racer track. Crashed his skull right in — as you saw.'

'Yes?' Grew raised the sheet again. 'Who was he?'

'My husband.'

The word came dispassionately from the carmined lips of the blonde woman. She stood up and walked towards Grew, showing the studied grace of a mannequin. The inspector did not miss the hint of contempt in her voice as she added, 'Trust Orlando to go out in a big way! He should have had the newsreel men notified.'

Grew dropped the sheet again and scrutinised in vain the woman's attractive though hardened features for some trace of emotion at her bereavement. 'And your name is?' he asked.

The woman shrugged. 'Mrs. Orlando Rival. My husband owned best part of the show out there. Guess it's mine now though.'

Grew felt sickened at the woman's blatant materialism. He turned abruptly to Duncan. 'This doesn't seem exactly to be my line of country, Doc.,' he said. 'Still, make out your report and send it to the station. I'll let you know about the inquest — '

'Just a moment, Inspector,' and the doctor, interrupting him, laid a hand on Grew's arm and propelled him gently towards the flap door. 'I'd like you to take a look at the place the body hit. I'd like your opinion on . . . '

His voice trailed away as the two of them reached the open air outside. Duncan walked on a few paces and then spoke confidentially, as Grew began to protest.

'Sorry to hustle you out like that, Inspector, but I don't trust those two in there. The woman anyway. A more callous specimen with her husband lying there dead — I've yet to meet. Seems almost as though she wanted the accident to happen.'

Grew peered at him in the semi-darkness. 'What are you getting at Doc? Didn't you yourself say — '

'I said apparently, Grew old man. Sure — the fellow's clothes reeked of whisky. Sure, his brains were knocked out when he hit that concrete pier. But — ' his voice grew suddenly tense ' — I'll stake my reputation that Rival was dead before he was put in that flying chair.'

Grew frowned. 'What makes you think so?'

'Lack of blood about the face and clothes of the corpse,' went on Duncan. laconically. 'Should have been plastered with it. There is only a smudge or two on the concrete too. Course it may be a freak case but I've a hunch I'm right.'

'But Doc — ' protested Grew, 'are you seriously asking me to believe that whoever did it dragged Rival's body through all that crowd and in full view propped him into position on the chair-o-plane? It doesn't make sense.'

'Yes it does,' said Duncan quietly, 'if the murderer pretended Rival was drunk. Besides there's only a crowd around two-thirds of the chair-o-plane machine. The other part faces the racer pillars and the fringe of caravans. He could have slipped on to that platform from this side without probably meeting a soul. Especially — in the dark.'

Grew laughed. 'What d'you mean, in the dark? There's a chain of arc-lamps all round the thing. If the crowd in front didn't see him the people in the other chairs waiting for the machine to start off would have.'

'*Not in the dark*,' persisted the doctor with a faint smile noticeable around his rather full lips. 'You see, Inspector — I've been doing a spot of detective work on my own before you arrived. I found out from the youth in charge of the chair-o-planes that there was a current failure here just before his machine started on that fatal trip. Said he had collected all the fares and had just pulled the lever to start the machine when everything blacked out. Only lasted a minute or two he said, and he didn't check up on his fares again when the machine started off again. Didn't even notice Rival was aboard.'

Grew thought over the information, all the while stroking the ends of his waxed, full moustache. 'Certainly might have happened at that,' he admitted grudgingly at last. 'It all depends on whether that

70

hunch of yours about Rival being dead when he was put on the machine works out.' He sighed, and looked at his watch. 'That means a post-mortem and probably, dragging old Fortescue the police surgeon out of bed. Will his face be red! Though nothing like mine'll be — if it's a false alarm.'

'Stake my life on it,' repeated the doctor as they began walking back to the tent. 'Though if you're sceptical — why not let me do the post-mortem and save Fortesque the trouble? I could get started straight away.'

Grew smiled. 'Thanks, Doc — that's nice of you, but regulations are regulations. Forty's the police surgeon and he'll have to do the job. Thanks for offering all the same.'

Back once more inside the small tent, Grew sent one of his sergeants to telephone Fortescue and for an ambulance.

Duncan chipped in here. 'The ambulance is already here, Inspector. Been standing by for almost half an hour until you arrived.'

'All right Fred.' Grew revised his

instructions to the sergeant. 'Tell 'em to get cracking. Fortescue likes to work at St. Annes so they better take the body there. Now — ' he turned towards the blonde woman and her companion who were again seated at the baize table. 'Do you feel up to answering a few questions, or has the evening proved too much of an ordeal for you?'

Sarcasm was also against regulations, but as he looked at the woman, Grew couldn't help it. Her reply showed that his little taunts had fallen on a skin tougher than he'd ever met before.

'Ordeal? That's a laugh!' the woman scoffed. 'I tell you, copper — first thing I'm gonna do tomorrow is to get good and drunk by way of celebration! Ordeal!' She scoffed again, then looked knowingly across at the check-suited man. 'Ain't I bin prayin' six years for something like this to happen, Paul? Ain't I?'

The check-suited man, florid of face and sporting a dapper moustache raised his obviously clipped eyebrows uneasily. 'How the hell do I know what you've bin praying for six years, Mave! Course I know you'n' Orlando didn't get on too well — but you didn't oughta talk like you're doing — with him just dead. It — it ain't decent.'

'Just who are you — ' interrupted Grew, ' — and what's your connection here in this business?'

The man in the check suit threw down his cigar-butt and ground it with a tan-heeled shoe into the sawdust sprinkled on the floor of the tent. His dark eyes looked up at the Inspector unwaveringly.

'My name's Rimmer. I'm sitting here right this moment on account of I'm an old friend of Mave's. And because I run that part of the show outside that don't belong to Orlando.'

'You mean — you're his partner?'

Rimmer shook his head. 'Nope. I mean that he was the big boss and I was a smaller one — that's all.'

'I see.' Grew stroked his moustache again. 'Was your relationship — er — cordial?'

Rimmer shrugged. 'We kept apart most times. But — '

'You make me sick, Paul.' The woman

Mave suddenly broke in glaring at Rimmer. 'You and your 'it ain't decent'! You know damn well you hated Orlando's guts every bit as much as I did. Ever since that poker game years ago — '

'Why don't you keep your mouth shut, Mave!' Rimmer had half-risen from his seat. 'The cops aren't interested in me. It's you they're questioning — ' he glared at Duncan, the sergeant at the door flap and back to the Inspector. 'I don't want no part of it, see!'

'For God's sake — what am I tellin'?' went on the woman unabashed. 'Nothing that ain't common gossip out front there among the show people! They all know you used to own this whole set-up, lock stock and barrel, and lost most of it to Orlando in a poker game! That afterwards you found the game was crooked and swore to get even with him one day!' She shrugged. 'Well — he's dead now, and I for one can't say I'm sorry.'

As she was speaking Grew saw the dull flush of anger rising in Rimmer's coarse cheeks, and the man's bullish neck tightened with strain, then relaxed again as the man apparently mastered his rage. Grew addressed him.

'Is what Mrs. Rival says true?'

Riinmer sighed, then nodded. 'Yep. Though I don't see what concern it is of yours. I was a sucker once and I paid for it.' He glared at Grew with a strange intensity. 'That's all the business I ever did with — with Orlando.'

'H'm.' Inspector Grew frowned. Why was the chap so touchy about being associated with the dead man? Unless of course he knew for certain something that Grew himself wasn't yet sure of. That Orlando Rival had in fact been murdered. Grew took out his notebook and made an entry, then faced the woman again. 'So — your late husband was a gambler, Mrs. Rival. Was that why you — er, 'didn't get on' with him?'

Mave Rival laughed derisively. 'Gambler isn't quite the word. Orlando played cards — but never lost unless it suited his book. Which ain't surprising when you remember he was the 'King of Illusions' before the bottom dropped out of variety shows in this country. He could deal himself four aces — and the joker — any time he pleased, and make it look natural. No.' She drew in her breath sharply, and as she went on, Grew detected for the first time some hint of real emotion in her voice. 'It was his women that upset me.'

Grew coughed. 'You mean — '

'I mean he'd chase any goddamn little slut that gave him the 'come-on' and plenty that didn't!' There was hatred, loathing and humiliation springing from the woman in a torrent as she half-shouted the words, her bosom heaving. 'Then he'd come back and taunt me — brag about every filthy rotten little detail — until sometimes I — I — '

Despite himself, Inspector Grew was beginning to feel the least bit sorry for his earlier sarcasm when an interruption — in the form of the ambulance attendants — cut short the woman's hysterical outburst. Grew superintended the moving of the body then, with Duncan, bade the two show-folk good night. There was nothing more he could do until he had Fortescue's report.

As they walked through the now

deserted, litter-strewn fun fair, the doctor, in answer to Grew's questions, recited once again the main details of the accident. He detailed the two sergeants to take statements from whatever witnesses they could find amongst the fairground operators, and finally accepted the offer of a lift in Duncan's grey sports car as far as St. Annes mortuary.

The night sky was clear now and silent as they drove back along the esplanade. Grew, his mind busy with possibilities, gazed unseeingly as bright moonlight poured its quicksilver over the white pebble beach and the dark murmuring plain of the sea itself. Money — won or lost at cards — and women. Two pretty substantial reasons for a possible murder motive. And two pretty tough-looking suspects — though he doubted whether the woman single-handed could have pulled off the job — if, indeed, it was murder. Though together, they might have —

'By the way, Grew, old chap, I haven't seen you up at the Country Club lately,' Duncan interrupted the police officer's train of thought. 'What's the matter — too much crime in this little town?'

Grew laughed. 'You doctors!' he said with a grin. 'All you think about is playing golf or bridge or potting at clay pigeons. If you had to do a real day's work —'

The swish of brakes as Duncan brought the car to a stop outside St. Annes ended the good-natured bantering. Grew thanked the doctor for his help and walked slowly up the cement steps in front of the hospital building to where a sole light glowed in an outside porch. He'd just wait for Fortesque's report and then call it a day.

As he waited on a hard wooden bench outside the post-mortem theatre, Grew found himself wondering how he had come by a large smudge of damp, reddish-brown mud that was adhering to the side of his coat. As he brushed it off he figured he'd picked it up somewhere at the pleasure ground — from one of the booths or in the marquee.

'Inspector!'

Grew looked up to see Fortescue, a wiry, saturnine little man in a white operating smock, beckoning to him.

Grew, crossing to the door of the room, saw that beneath his hard-bitten exterior, the police surgeon was literally simmering with excitement.

'It was murder!' he said as Grew reached him. 'Very ingenious too. Come inside.'

★ ★ ★

Next morning Grew breakfasted early, and, after a brief talk to Superintendent Hurton on the telephone, studied his sergeants' reports as the squad car took him again towards the fairground. The information contained in the reports was indeed meagre and he snorted in disgust.

'H'mph.' He waved the sheets of paper derisively. 'Not a darn thing of use. Why do people walk around with their eyes shut.'

Sergeant Watson, crouching over the wheel grimaced. 'Usually the way, chief — when anything is happening. Or — maybe it's just their tongues that want loosening. We gathered the idea they were sort of 'hanging together'.'

'That so?' Grew started drawing at an old briar pipe. 'Maybe they won't be so keen when they find out it may be a case of hanging from the gallows. You'd be surprised how that helps people to remember things . . . '

'So it was murder then chief?' ventured Sergeant Dooley from the back seat.

'Yes. Rival was shot through the eye with a small-bore rifle. Probably a .22 Winchester,' supplied the Inspector. 'Pretty neat job — by an expert marksman. No blood. No fuss. Fortescue had a hard job finding the slug, which was lodged in the back of Rival's skull.' Grew drew on his pipe again. 'Bloke who did this was too clever. The very lack of blood was a dead give-away. Doctor Duncan spotted it first when he called us up, and so did Fortescue. That was why he kept trying when he found no poison or other effects inside the body. So your first job, boys, today is to round up every rifle from the shooting galleries in the fairground.'

'You mean — ' put in Sergeant-driver Watson as the black car swung into the esplanade once more ' — you think it was done with one of 'the four shots a shilling' guns?'

'Sticks out a mile doesn't it, my lad?' countered the Inspector. 'They're pretty accurate up to ten-twenty yards; and easy to get hold of for anyone in the business.' He tamped out his pipe and put it in his pocket. 'Manton — of the forensic lab — has the slug for photographing. I want you to take him all the rifles you pick up — there'll probably be thirty or forty of 'em — and stand by. Things'll look pretty sticky for whoever was in charge of the gun that killed Rival.'

'But, chief — ' it was Dooley again ' — couldn't it have been an accident after all? I mean Rival could ha' sat himself in that chair-o-plane and been killed by a stray shot from one of the rifles.'

Grew scowled. 'You *would* think of that, Sam,' he snorted, 'but I don't think so. It'd be something more than a million to one against!'

★ ★ ★

At the fairground, Inspector Grew was met by Jerry Trent of the fingerprints department who had come on instructions from Superintendent Hurton. Leaving Dooley and Watson on their quest for rifles, Grew and his companion first made for the mechanic in charge of the electric power installation that had so mysteriously failed to function at the critical moment.

He turned out to be the tow-headed, uncivil youth Grew had first set eyes on the night before, and was apparently unable to add anything to his statement which simply was that ' . . . someone had thrown out the main switch and I just pushed it in again and everything was okay.' He hadn't seen or heard anything or anybody mysterious. Mr. Rimmer had however, come up just afterwards to ask what was the big idea, putting the lights out.

'Rimmer, eh?' Grew noted the fact.

The youth nodded. 'Sure. He was pretty sore. Told me to be more careful or I'd have trouble on me hands.'

'What exactly did he mean by that?'

'Aw — ' the youth shrugged ' — he had

a bee in his bonnet about it bein' dangerous with the lights out. Y'see he runs that string o' shooting galleries across there. He was scared someone might walk in front of a bullet or somethin' in the dark.'

'He was, was he?' Grew looked knowingly at Trent, who raised his eyebrows in mute reply. 'Well, Jerry my lad — ' He pointed to the square ebonite switchboard gleaming with switches, from which the current was distributed. ' — cover every inch of that for prints. If you want me I'll be with Mrs. Rival.'

The youth conducted him to a luxurious motor-caravan, which was apparently the Rivals' living quarters. The square marquee, the youth explained, had been Orlando's office.

Mave Rival, in answer to the Inspector's knock, bade him enter and make himself at home while she finished dressing in a partitioned-off end of the caravan. Grew did as was bid, all the time his keen eyes were taking stock of the interior. It was furnished in execrable taste, with red plush and gilt images mingling with brass knick-knacks and string bead curtains.

He looked more closely at a series of pin-ups of what had obviously been Mave Rival years ago together with her fair-haired husband. Then suddenly Grew found himself staring pop-eyed at one picture which showed the woman dressed in 'cowgirl' costume hugging a rifle to her shoulder. There was a cut-out caption, beneath which read 'The Queen of the Rifle — See Her Shoot The Cigarette From Her Lover's Lips!'

So . . . Mave Rival was a crack rifle shot! And Rimmer owned a string of shooting galleries. In addition they both hated Orlando Rival like hell! There seemed to be scope there for closer examination of both of their movements, the night before.

Nevertheless, after Grew's statement of the real cause of her husband's death, Mave Rival, though awed and somewhat shaken, stuck to a story that she had been in her caravan all the evening. Grew could check up — if he cared — with one of the show women who was with her most of the time. Rimmer, however, when called, was much vaguer. Said he'd been right out of the fairground, walking along the shore most of the evening and didn't get back until the accident had happened.

When Grew broke him down, however, with the mechanic's story of the lights incident, Mave Rival came to the rescue.

'You might as well know, copper,' she said incisively. 'Paul was in there with me. Orlando spun me a yarn about going out to a club or somethin' — but I knew that meant another woman. So I invited Paul in. We're sort of — old friends — if you know what I mean. I'll swear he didn't leave me until those lights went! He didn't have nothin' to do with — with anything — '

'That'll be for me to decide, Mrs. Rival,' said Grew grimly, 'when I find out which gun killed your husband. If it's one of yours, Rimmer — the pair of you'll have some more explaining to do. So — better not try any tricks. I'll be in to see you again this afternoon!'

★ ★ ★

Some four hours later, after lunch, Manton, the ballistics expert, called on Grew at the station. All the rifles collected — Winchester .22s — had been useless, because the slug from Rival's brain had proved to be a .24.

'Most unusual calibre,' wound up Manton. 'German or Italian I should think. They use it quite a lot.'

'Mph,' grunted the inspector, then flipped across the desk a small cartridge shell. 'Anything like that one?'

Manton fingered the shell for a moment, then nodded. 'Yes! Very definitely. Where'd you get it?'

'Fell from the cuff of the dead man's trousers this morning. I — excuse me.' he broke off as his telephone began ringing. He answered it, listened for some moments then said. 'Nice work, Fred. Keep on his tail and report anything suspicious.' He hung up then turned back to Manton. 'Our friend Rimmer seems to be having an afternoon off,' he said easily. 'Just gone up to the County Club.'

'The club?' queried Manton rubbing his chin. 'Well — that's pretty calm — for a man with a. possible murder rap hanging over his head. Unless — by George!' he snapped his fingers ' — I forgot. The rifle range there — in the old sandpit. There's a gunroom too, with lockers for the use of members to keep their guns in.'

'You mean — ' put in Grew ' — if Rimmer wanted a safe hiding place he'd put it in that gunroom — where no one'd think of looking! I believe you've got something there. Supposing we, too, take the afternoon off eh?'

'Sure thing, Inspector. Let's get cracking.'

They were on the point of leaving the station when Dooley arrived from the fairground. With some excitement he put into Grew's arms a dark raincoat that had been discovered, rolled hastily underneath the chair-o-plane platform.

'I thought maybe it was shoved there on the quick by the murderer,' explained the sergeant. 'It was right where he would have come through from the caravans — and there was this note in one pocket.'

Grew took the paper he was holding

out and read: *This is your last chance. Either you pay up or I'll expose you to you know who —*

The note ended with a torn edge. 'Thanks, Sam,' said Grew. He eyed the raincoat, noted that it was liberally splashed with reddish brown mud. Somewhere he'd seen that reddish brown before. Of course! Last night . . .

Slowly he went over in his mind the events of last evening, recalling as near as he could every incident and conversation. Then a grim smile began to curve his lips. He turned to Manton. 'Can we use your car, old man, for that trip to the Country Club? More than ever now — I've a hunch the answer to all our troubles lies in that gunroom. And maybe — the card room there too!'

★ ★ ★

Late that evening the funfair at Long-beach was at its height. Inspector Grew, with the Superintendent and sergeants Watson and Dooley under cover of darkness ranged themselves in the rear of the chair-o-plane machine. The Inspector had completed his case — all but arresting the murderer — and had persuaded the Super to let him finish the case his way and catch the suspect red handed.

'When the guilty party realises we know it was murder — they'll come back for that raincoat. All we have to do is to watch and wait — ah. Here comes someone. Ready, men!'

From the darkness among the caravans came the shuffle of stealthy footsteps. A figure crept furtively nearer. Then Grew shouted an order as the figure swerved towards the switchboard below the steam traction engine and the lights were once again extinguished. Amid the screams and shouts that came from the pleasure fair at this debacle, Grew saw Dooley and Watson fling themselves forward in the darkness and go rolling over on the grass. Grew jumped to his feet and threw in the switch again, and smiled grimly as he saw that the sergeants had got their man.

'Nice work, boys.' he congratulated, and gazed at the scowling figure between them who was tugging at the handcuffs they had lost no time in slipping on. 'Nice evening too — for reclaiming your raincoat — eh, Doctor Duncan? Perhaps you'll be good enough to accept a lift in my car this time . . .'

Later that evening, Grew explained to Watson and Dooley the events that led up to him suspecting the doctor.

'Right up until the time you turned in that raincoat, Sam, I was working in the dark. I strongly suspected Rimmer and the Rival woman. Specially when I found out that she was a crack shot with a small-bore gun. They both had cast-iron motives and rotten alibis. Either or both could have done it — given the opportunity. That was where I became stuck. Because this Rival gent knew exactly how both of them felt about him — and he'd have run a mile as soon as he'd seen either of them anywhere near with a rifle looking like business.

'Then Rimmer took it into his head to go to the country club, and Manton recalled the shooting range there, and the gun lockers; but I, more than anything, saw the red mud on that coat, and recalled that the Club rifle range was situated in an old sandpit full of the stuff. Then I checked again the toe-caps of Rival's shoes — and they too, were covered with it, as though his limp body had been dragged through this reddish mud perhaps to a car.'

'That means,' said Watson, 'you fixed the place where the crime was committed. The sand pit, while probably both Duncan and Rival were shooting, but what made you connect Duncan with Rival? There was no name in the coat or on the note?'

Grew smiled. 'Red mud again, my lad. I found some on my own coat last night while I was waiting at St. Annes for Fortescue's verdict on the *post-mortem*. I wondered where I'd picked it up, the more so when today I particularly noticed up at the fairground the earth was quite ordinarily black. So — there could have been only one place I *could* have picked it up — in Duncan's car. Remember — he gave me that lift down, while you were staying on taking statements?'

'Well — I'm darned,' grinned Sergeant Watson. ' — And you mean that little bit of mud really meant all that much?'

'It meant a lot. Fred Manton and I went up to the Club though, as arranged. Rimmer saw us, and left — he was playing in the card room. Then I had a word with the club steward who told me a thing or two. Apparently Duncan had recently been losing heavily at cards. Imagine my surprise when I found out to whom.'

'Rival?' guessed Dooley.

'Yes. He and Rimmer joined the place years ago, when they were fairly good friends. Since they fell out, Rival gave the place a miss until a year or so ago. Then Duncan attended him one night for a slight illness, the men became friends and Rival began to use the place again.

'However, to get back to this afternoon,' went on Grew. 'I thanked the steward and went with Manton down to the gunroom. Rimmer had a gun there and so had Duncan. We examined them both. Rimmer's was an ordinary .22 Winchester but Duncan's was just the one we were looking for. A .24 Remmger — a German make now almost obsolete. All that remained was to photograph the rifling and compare it with the slug from Rival's skull. While Manton was checking up on that I too checked up on Duncan and found that he had indeed been up to the range the day before and taken out his gun. The man in charge of the locker-room remembered particularly because it was such a filthy day that no other member had bothered to turn out. The attendant said that he gave Duncan a supply of target-cards and saw him drive off towards the range, which is a half-mile or so away from the clubhouse and entirely hidden from view by trecs. The man also thought he saw someone else in the car but couldn't be sure.'

'But why, chief,' asked Dooley, 'should Rival have wanted to go shooting on such a filthy day? He wasn't a very sporting kind of gent so far as I could see.'

'That's one point. Duncan cleared up for me — he made a full confession after we took him back to the station. He said that it was to give him a chance to clear his bet with Rival. He owed him a large sum, and he dared Rival to wager it double or quits on a shooting match. Rival shot first and made a ninety-five per cent score. Duncan's hopes faded, and he could envisage only exposure and ruin now doubly certain. Rival was standing near the target to notch the shots, so instead of aiming for the bullseye Duncan aimed at Rival's . . . And hit it,' he finished laconically. 'Then carried the body down here — and well you know the rest.'

'Then why — ' persisted Watson, ' — did he go to all the trouble to call in the police and tell you he thought it was murder?'

'Because,' said Grew with a tolerant sigh, 'as I told you he'd been too clever. He knew at once that any doctor would see Rival hadn't met his death through hitting that wall, no matter how convincingly he'd been propped into one of those chair-o-plane seats. So Duncan tries to go one better, by asking if he can do the *post-mortem*. He thinks that if he can get hold of that slug from Rival's skull no one'll ever be able to make a case out against him. He'd have been right too. So you see, you lads,' Grew finished up paternally, stroking his waxed moustache-ends with a flourish ' — police regulations sometimes come in useful. If it hadn't have been for them, Duncan would have had the *post-mortem* job — and I might have been looking for a new one for not solving a pretty clean-cut case of murder. Now you can drive me home, Fred my lad. I want a nice early night tonight.'

'Well — I'm afraid you're not going to have it chief,' said driver Watson with a grin, as a message came through the car radio at that moment. 'There's a call going out now. Someone's started a 'free-for-all' on the Palace Pier . . . '

4

Wanderer of Time

Professor Hardwick once delivered a learned lecture to a group of earnest students.

'Time does not exist in actual fact,' Professor Hardwick had said. 'It is simply the term science applies to a condition of space which it does not fully comprehend. We know that there has been a Past, and can prove it; we also know that there is a Future, but we cannot prove it. Therein lies the need for the term 'Time,' in order that an insurmountable difficulty may become resolved into common understanding.'

This excerpt from his paper — a pedantic observation without doubt — had prompted Blake Carson, spare-time dabbler in physics, to think further. Much further. He had heard Hardwick make that statement five years ago. Now Hardwick was dead, but every observation he had ever made, every treatise he had written, had been absorbed to the full by the young physicist. Between the ages of twenty-five and thirty he had plowed through the deeper works of Einstein, Eddington, and Jeans to boot.

'Time,' Blake Carson observed, to his little laboratory, when the five years had gone by, 'definitely does not exist! It is a concept engendered by the limitations of a physical body. And a physical body, according to Eddington and Jeans, is the outward manifestation of thought itself. Change the thought and you change the body in like proportion. You believe you know the past. So adjust your mind to the situation and there is no reason why you shouldn't know the future.'

Two years later he added an amendment.

'Time is a circle, in which thought itself and all its creations go in an everlasting cycle, repeating the process without end. Therefore, if we have in a remote past done the same things we are doing now, it is logical to assume that some hangover of memory may be left behind — a hangover from the past which, from the present standpoint, will be in the future, so far back is it in the time circle.

'The medium for thought is the brain. Therefore, any hangover must be in the brain. Find that, and you have the key to future time. All you will actually do will be to awake a memory of the remote past.'

From this conception there sprouted in Blake Carson's laboratory a complicated mass of apparatus contrived from hard-earned savings and erected in spare time. Again and again he built and rebuilt, tested and experimented, finally got assistance from two other young men with ideas similar to his own. They did not fully understand his theory but his enthusiasm certainly impressed them.

At last he had things exactly as he wanted them, summoned his two friends one Saturday evening and waved a hand to his apparatus.

Dick Glenbury was shock-haired, ruddy-faced, and blue-eyed — a man of impulses, honesty, and dependable concentration. Hart Cranshaw was the exact opposite

— sallow-skinned, always unruffled, black-haired. A brilliant physicist, confirmed cynic, with only his great intelligence to save him from being a complete bore.

'Boys, I have it,' Blake Carson declared with enthusiasm, grey eyes gleaming. 'You know my theory regarding the hangover. This' — he motioned to the apparatus — 'is the Probe.'

'You don't mean you intend to use all this stuff on your brain to probe for the right spot, do you?' Dick Glenbury demanded.

'That is the idea, yes.'

'When you've done this, what then?' Cranshaw asked, sticking to the practical side, as usual.

'Tell you better when I know something,' Carson grinned. 'Right now I want you to follow out instructions.'

He seated himself in the chair immediately under the wilderness of odd-looking lenses, lamps, and tubes. Following directions Glenbury busied himself with the switchboard. One projector gave forth a violet ray that enveloped Blake Carson's head completely.

Opposite him, so he could see it clearly, a squared and numbered screen came into life and gave a perfect silhouette, X-ray wise, of his skull. It differed only from X-ray in that the convolutions of the brain were clearly shown more vividly than any other part.

'There,' Carson gasped abruptly. 'Look in Section Nine, Square Five. There's a black oval mark — a blind spot. No registration at all. That is a hangover.'

He pressed a switch on the chair arm.

'Taking a photograph,' he explained. Then giving the order to cut off the entire apparatus, he got to his feet. Within a few minutes he had produced a finished print, which he handed round in obvious delight.

'So what?' Cranshaw growled, his sallow face mystified. 'Now you have got a blind spot what good does it do you? All this is way outside the physics I ever learned. You still can't see the future.' This last was added with some impatience.

'But I shall.' Carson's voice was tense. 'You notice that that blind spot is exactly where we might expect it to be? In the subconscious area. To get a clear knowledge of what the spot contains there is only one method to use.'

'Yeah.' Glenbury said grimly. 'A surgeon should link up the blank portion with the active portion of your brain by means of a nerve. And would that be a ticklish business.'

'I don't need a surgeon,' Carson said. 'Why a real nerve? A nerve is only a fleshly means of carrying minute electrical sensation. A small electric device can do it just as well. In other words an external mechanical nerve.'

He turned aside and brought forth an object not unlike a stethoscope. At both ends were suction caps and small dry batteries. Between the caps was a length of strong cable.

'A brain gives off minute electric charges — anybody knows that,' Carson resumed. 'This mechanical device can accomplish the thing through the skull bone. Thereby the blind spot and normal brain area would be linked. At least that's how I figure it.'

'Well, all right,' Dick Glenbury said, with an uneasy glance at Hart Cranshaw. 'To me it sounds like a novel way of committing suicide.'

'Like suffocating in your own waste,' Cranshaw agreed.

'If you weren't so fact-bound you'd see my point,' Blake snorted. 'Anyway, I'm going to try it.'

Again he switched on his brain-reading equipment, studied the screen and the photograph for a moment, then he clamped one end of the artificial nerve device onto his skull. The other suction cup he moved indecisively about his head, positioning it by watching it on the screen. Time and again he fished round the blind spot, finally pressed the cap home.

A sensation of crawling sickness passed through him as though his body were being slowly turned inside out. His laboratory, the tense faces of Glenbury and Cranshaw misted mysteriously and were gone. Images as though reflected from disturbed water rippled through his brain.

An inchoate mass of impressions slammed suddenly into his consciousness. There were scurrying people superimposed on ragged cliffs, against which plunged foaming seas. From the cliffs there seemed to sprout the towers of an unknown, remote, incomparably beautiful city catching the light of an unseen sun. Machines — people — mists. A thundering, grinding pain . . .

He opened his eyes suddenly to find himself sprawled on the laboratory floor with brandy scorching his throat.

'Of all the darned, tomfool experiments,' Dick Glenbury exploded. 'You went out like a light after the first few minutes.'

'I told you it was no use,' Cranshaw snorted. 'The laws of physics are against this kind of thing. Time is locked up — '

'No, Hart, it isn't.' Carson stirred on the floor and rubbed his aching head. 'Definitely it isn't,' he insisted.

Getting to his feet he stared before him dreamily.

'I saw the future!' he whispered. 'It wasn't anything clear — but it must have been the future. There was a city such as we have never imagined. Everything was cross-sectioned, like a montage. The reason for that was my own inaccuracy with the artificial nerve. Next time I'll do better.'

'Next time?' Cranshaw echoed. 'You're going on with this risk? It might even kill you before you're through.'

'Perhaps,' Carson admitted, in a quiet voice. He shrugged. 'Pioneers have often paid dearly for their discoveries. But I have a key. I'm going on, boys, until it swings wide open.'

For months afterwards Blake Carson became absorbed in his experiments. He gave up his ordinary work, lived on what savings he had and went tooth and nail after his discovery.

At first he was elated by the precision and accuracy with which he could achieve results. Then as days passed both Hart Cranshaw and Dick Glenbury noticed that an odd change had come over him, for he seemed morose, afraid of letting some statement or other escape him.

'What is it, Blake?' Dick Glenbury

insisted one evening, when he had arrived for the latest report on progress. 'You're different. Something is on your mind. You can surely tell me, your best friend.'

As Blake Carson smiled, Glenbury suddenly noticed how tired he looked.

'Which doesn't include Hart, eh?' Carson asked.

'I didn't mean that exactly. But he is a bit cold-blooded when it comes to truths. What's wrong?'

'I have discovered when I am to die,' Blake Carson said soberly.

'So what? We all die sometime.' Dick Glenbury stopped uneasily. There was a strange look on Blake Carson's worn face.

'Yes, we all die sometime, of course, but I shall go one month hence. On April fourteenth. And I shall die in the electric chair for first-degree murder.'

Dick Glenbury stared, appalled. 'What! You, a murderer? Why, it's utterly — say, that artificial nerve has gone cockeyed.'

'I'm afraid not, Dick,' answered Carson. 'I realize now that death ends this particular phase of existence on this plane. The views of the future that I have seen refer to some other plane ways beyond this, the plane where successive deaths would ultimately carry me. With death, all association with things here is broken.'

'I still don't believe murder is ahead of you,' Dick Glenbury said.

'None the less I shall die as a convicted murderer,' Carson went on, his voice harsh. 'The man who gets me into this approaching mess and who will have the perfect alibi is — Hart Cranshaw.'

'Hart? You mean he is going to commit a murder deliberately and blame you for it?'

'Without doubt. We know already that he is interested now in this invention of mine; we know too that he realizes he has a blind spot in his brain, just as everybody else has. Hart, cold-blooded and calculating, sees the value of this invention to gain power and control for himself. Stock markets, gambling speculations, history before it appears. He could even rule the world. He will steal the secret from me and rid himself of the only two men in the world who know of his villainy.'

'The only two men?' repeated Glenbury. 'You mean I, also, will be slain?'

'Yes.' Blake Carson's voice had a far away sound.

'But this can't happen,' Glenbury shouted huskily. 'I'm not going to — to be murdered just to further the aims of Hart Cranshaw. Like blazes I am! You forget, Blake — forewarned is forearmed. We can defeat this.' his voice became eager. 'Now that we know about it, we can take steps to block him.'

'No,' Carson interrupted. 'I've had many weeks to think this over, Dick — weeks that have nearly driven me mad as I realized the truth. The law of time is inexorable. It must happen! Don't you even yet realize that all I have seen is only an infinitely remote memory from a past time, over which moments we are passing again? All this has happened before. You will be murdered as surely as I knew you would come here tonight, and I shall die convicted of that murder.'

Dick Glenbury's face had gone the colour of putty. 'When does it happen?'

'At exactly nine minutes after eleven

tonight — here.' Carson paused and gripped Glenbury's shoulders tightly. 'Stars above, Dick, can't you realize how all this hurts me, how frightful it is for me to have to tell it all to you. It's only because I know you're a hundred percent that I spoke at all.'

'Yes — I know.' Glenbury sank weakly into a chair. For a moment or two his mind wandered. Next he found that his frozen gaze was fixed on the electric clock. It was exactly forty minutes past ten.

'At ten to eleven — in ten minutes, that is — Hart will come here,' Carson resumed. 'His first words will be — 'Sorry I'm late, boys, but I got held up at an Extraordinary Board Meeting.' An argument will follow, then murder. Everything is clear up to the moment of my death. After that Hart is extinguished from my future. The vision of life continuing in a plane different from this one is something I have pondered pretty deeply.'

Dick Glenbury did not speak, but Carson went on, musing aloud. 'Suppose,' Carson said, 'I was to try an experiment with time? Suppose, because I possess knowledge no man has ever had so far — I were able to upset the order of the Circle. Suppose, I came back, after I have been electrocuted, to confront Hart with your murder and my wrongful execution?'

'No,' Glenbury's mind was too lethargic to take things in.

'I've already told you that the body obeys the mind. Normally, at my death, I shall recreate my body in a plane removed from this one. But suppose my thoughts upon the moment of death are entirely concentrated on returning to this plane at a date one week after execution? That would be April twenty-first. I believe I might thereby return to confront Hart.'

'Do you know you can do this?'

'No; but it seems logical to assume that I can. Since the future, after death, is on another plane, I cannot tell whether my plan would work or not. As I have told you, Hart ceases to be in my future time from the moment I die, unless I can change the course of Time and thereby do something unique. I guess I — '

Carson broke off as the door opened suddenly and Hart Cranshaw came in. He threw down his hat casually.

'Sorry I'm late, boys, but I got held up at an Extraordinary Board Meeting — ' He broke off. 'What's wrong, Dick? Feeling faint?'

Dick Glenbury did not answer. He was staring at the clock. It was exactly ten minutes to eleven.

'He's okay,' Blake Carson said quietly, turning. 'Just had a bit of a shock, that's all. I've been taking a look into the future, Hart, and I've discovered plenty that isn't exactly agreeable.'

'Oh?' Hart Cranshaw looked thoughtful for a moment, then went on, 'Matter of fact, Blake, it strikes me that I've been none too cordial towards you considering the brilliance of the thing you have achieved. I'd like to know plenty more about this invention if you'd tell me.'

'Yes, so you can steal it!' Dick Glenbury shouted suddenly, leaping to his feet. 'That's your intention. The future has shown that to Blake already. And you'll try and kill me in the doing. But you're not going to. By heavens, no! So Time can't be cheated, Blake? We'll see about that.'

He raced for the door, but he did not reach it. Hart Cranshaw caught him by the arm and swung him back.

'What the devil are you raving about?' he snapped. 'Do you mean to say I intend to murder you?'

'That is why you came here, Hart,' Carson declared quietly. 'Time doesn't lie, and all your bluster and pretended innocence makes not the least difference to your real intentions. You figure to do plenty with this invention of mine.'

'All right, supposing I do?' Hart Cranshaw snapped, suddenly whipping an automatic from his pocket. 'What are you going to do about it?'

Blake Carson shrugged. 'Only what immutable law makes me do!'

'To blazes with this!' Dick Glenbury shouted suddenly. 'I'm not standing here obeying immutable laws — not when my life's in danger. Hart, drop that gun!'

Hart Cranshaw only grinned frozenly. In desperation Glenbury dived for him, caught his foot in a snaking cable on the floor and collided with the physicist. Whether it was accident or design Blake Carson could not be sure at the moment, but the automatic certainly exploded.

Hart Cranshaw stood in momentary silence as Dick Glenbury slid gently to the floor and lay still. Blake Carson's eyes shifted to the clock — eleven-nine!

At length Hart Cranshaw seemed to recover himself. He held his automatic more firmly.

'Okay, Blake, you know the future, so you may as well know the rest — '

'I do,' Blake Carson interrupted him. 'You are going to pin this thing on me. You shot Dick deliberately.'

'Not deliberately: it was an accident. It just happened to come sooner than I'd figured, that's all. With both of you out of the way what is to prevent me becoming even the master of the whole world with this gadget of yours? Nothing!' Hart Cranshaw gave a grim smile. 'I planned it all out, Blake. For tonight I have a cast-iron alibi. It will be your task to prove yourself innocent of Dick Glenbury's murder.'

'I won't succeed: I know that already.'

Hart Cranshaw eyed him queerly. 'Considering what I have done — and what I am going to do — you're taking it mighty calmly.'

'Why not? Knowledge of the future makes one know what is inescapable — for both of us.' Blake Carson spoke the last words significantly.

'I've checked on my future already and I know darn well I'm in for a good time,' Hart Cranshaw retorted. He pondered for a moment then motioned with his gun. 'I'm taking no chances on you wrecking this machinery, Blake. I'd shoot you first and alibi myself out of it afterwards, only I don't want things to get too complicated. Grab the 'phone and call the police. Confess to them what you have done.'

With resigned calm Blake Carson obeyed. When he was through Hart Cranshaw nodded complacently.

'Good. Before the police arrive I'll be gone, leaving you this gun to explain away. Since I have kept my gloves on it puts me in the clear for fingerprints even though there won't be any of yours about. Just the same only you and Dick have been here together tonight. I have been elsewhere. I can prove it.'

Blake Carson smiled grimly. 'Then later you will pose as my sympathetic friend, will offer to look after my work while I am in custody, and save yourself by good lawyers and your cast-iron alibi. That's clever, Hart. But remember, to everything there is an appointed time!'

'Right now,' Hart Cranshaw answered in his conceited assured tones, 'the future looks quite rosy so far as I am concerned . . . '

Inevitably the law enacted every incident Blake Carson had already foreseen. Once in the hands of the police, cross-examined relentlessly, he saw all his chances of escape vanish. Carson was convicted of first-degree murder, and the Court pronounced the death sentence. The trial had proceeded in record time, as the murder was considered flagrant, and newspapers denounced Carson bitterly. To the horror of Carson's lawyer, he refused to take an appeal or resort to the usual methods of delay. Carson's attitude was fatalistic, and he could not be moved in his seeming determination to die.

In his cell Blake spent most of his time between sentence and execution brooding over the facts he had gleaned from his experiments. In thc death house in prison he was certainly a model prisoner, quiet, preoccupied, just a little grim. His whole being was as a matter of fact built up into one fierce, unwavering concentration — the date of April twenty-first. Upon his mastery of elemental forces at the point of death depended his one chance of changing the law of time and confronting Hart Cranshaw with the impossible, a return from death.

Not a word of his intentions escaped him. He was unbowed on the last morning, listened to the prison chaplain's brief words of solace in stony silence, then walked the short length of dun corridor, between guards, to the fatal chamber. He sat down in the death chair with the calm of a man about to preside over a meeting.

The buckles on the straps clinked a little, disturbing him.

He hardly realized what was going on in the sombre, dimly lighted place. If his mental concentration concerning April twenty-first had been strong before, now it had become fanatical. Rigid, perspiration streaming down his face with the urgency of his thoughts, he waited

He felt it then — the thrilling, binding, racking current as it nipped his vitals, then spread and spread into an infinite snapping anguish in which the world and the universe was a brief blazing hell of dissolution.

Then things were quiet — oddly quiet . . .

He felt as though he were drifting in a sea without substance — floating alone. His concentration was superseded now by a dawning wonder, indeed a striving to come to grips with the weird situation in which he found himself.

He had died — his body had — he was convinced of that. But now, to break these iron bands of paralysis, that was the need!

He essayed a sudden effort and with it everything seemed to come abruptly into focus. He felt himself snap out of the void of in-between into normal — or at least mundane — surroundings. He stirred slowly. He was still alone, lying on his back on a somber, chilly plain of reddish dust. It occasioned him passing surprise that he was still dressed in the thin cotton shirt and pants of a prisoner.

A biting chill in the air went suddenly to his marrow. He shuddered as he got to his feet and looked down at himself.

'Of course. I held my clothes in thought as much as my body, so they were bound to be recreated also . . .

Baffled, he stared about him. Overhead the sky was violet blue and powdered with endless hosts of stars. To the right was a frowning ridge of higher ground. And everywhere, red soil. Time — an infinitely long span — had passed.

With a half cry he turned and ran breathlessly towards the ridge, scrambled up the rubble-strewn slope quickly. At the top he paused, appalled.

A red sun, swollen to unheard-of size, was bisected by the far distant jagged horizon — a sun to whose edge the stars themselves seemed to reach. He was old now, unguessably old, his incandescent fires burned out.

'Millions of years, quintillions of years,' Blake Carson whispered, sitting down with a thump on an upturned rock and staring out over the drear, somber vastness. 'In heaven's name, what have I done? What have I done?'

He stared in front of him, forced himself by superhuman effort to think calmly. He had planned for one week beyond death. Instead he had landed here, at the virtual end of Earth's existence, where age was stamped on everything. It was in the scarcely moving sun which spoke of Earth's near-standstill from tidal drag. It was in the red soil, the ferrous oxide of extreme senility, the rusting of the metallic deposits in the ground itself. It was in the thin air that had turned the atmospheric heights violet-blue and made breathing a sheer agony.

And there was something else too apart from all this which Blake Carson had only just begun to realize. He could no longer see the future.

'I cheated the normal course of

after-death,' he mused. 'I did not move to a neighbouring plane there to resume a continuation of life, and neither did I move to April twenty-one as I should have done. It can only mean that at the last minute there was an unpredictable error. It is possible that the electricity from the chair upset my brain planning and shifted the focus of my thoughts so that I was hurled ahead, not one week — but to here. And with that mishap I also lost the power to visualize the future. Had I died by any other way but electricity there might not have been that mistake.'

He shuddered again as a thin, ice-charged wind howled dismally out of the desolate waste and stabbed him through and through. Stung into movements, once more, he got up. Protecting his face from the brief, slashing hurricane he moved further along the ridge and gazed out over the landscape from a different vantage. And from here there was a new view. Ruins, apparently.

He began to run to keep himself warm, until the thin air flogged his lungs to bursting point. At a jog trot he moved on towards the mighty, hardly moving sun, stopped at last within the shadow of a vast, eroded hall.

It was red like everything else. Within it were the ponderous remains of dust-smothered machinery, colossi of power long disused and forgotten. He stared at them, unable to fathom their smallest meaning. His gaze travelled further — to the crumbled ruins of mighty edifices of rusting metal in the rear. Terrace upon terrace, to the violet sky. Here it seemed was a rusting monument to Man's vanished greatness, with the inexplicable and massive engines as the secret of his power . . .

And Man himself? Gone to other worlds? Dead in the red dust? Blake Carson shook himself fiercely at the inescapable conviction of total loneliness. Only the stars, the sun, and the wind — that awful wind, moaning now softly through the ruins, sweeping the distant corner of the horizon into a mighty cloud that blacked out the brazen glitter of the northern stars.

Blake Carson turned at last. At the far end of the ruins his eye had caught a faint gleam of reflection from the crimson sun.

It shone like a diamond. Baffled, he turned and hurried towards it, found the distance was deceptive and that it was nearly two miles off. The nearer he came the more the brightness resolved itself into one of six massively thick glass domes some six feet in diameter.

In all there were eight of them dotted about a little plateau that had been scraped mainly free of rubble and stone. It resembled the floor of a crater with frowning walls of rock all round it. Mystified, Carson moved to the nearest dome and peered through.

In that moment he forgot the melancholy wind and his sense of desperate loneliness — for below was life! Teeming life! Not human life, admittedly, but at least something that moved. It took him a little while to adjust himself to the amazing thing he had discovered.

Perhaps two hundred feet below the dome, brightly lighted, was a city in miniature. It reminded him of a model city of the future he had once seen at an exposition. There were terraces, pedestrian tracks, towers, even aircraft. It was all there on an infinitely minute scale, and probably spread far under the earth out of his line of vision.

But the teeming hordes were — ants. Myriads of them. Not rushing about with the apparent aimlessness of his own time, but moving with a definable, ordered purpose. Ants in a dying world? Ants with their own city?

'Of course,' he whispered, and his breath froze the glass. 'Of course. The law of evolution — man to ant, and ant to bacteria. Science has always visualized that. This I could never have known about for the future I saw was not on this plane . . . '

And Hart Cranshaw? The scheme of vengeance? It seemed a remote plan now. Down here was company — intelligent ants who, whatever they might think of him, would perhaps at least talk to him, help him . . .

Suddenly he beat his fists mightily on the glass, shouted hoarsely.

There was no immediate effect. He beat again, this time frenziedly, and the scurrying hordes below suddenly paused in their movement as though uncertain.

Then they started to scatter madly like bits of dust blown by the wind.

'Open up!' he shouted. 'Open up. I'm freezing.'

He was not quite sure what happened then, but it seemed to him that he went a little mad. He had a confused, blurred notion of running to each dome in turn and battering his fists against its smooth, implacable surface.

Wind, an endless wind, had turned his blood to ice. At last he sank down on an out-jutting rock at the plateau edge, buried his head in his hands and shivered. An overpowering desire to go to sleep was upon him, but presently it passed as he became aware of new thoughts surging through his brain, mighty thoughts that were not his own.

He saw, in queer kaleidoscopic fashion, the ascent of man to supreme heights: he saw too man's gradual realization that he was upon a doomed world. He saw the thinning of the multitudes and the survival of the fittest — the slow, inexorable work of Nature as she adapted life to suit her latest need.

Like a panorama of the ages, hurdling great vistas of time, Blake Carson saw the human body change into that of the termite, of which the termite of his own time was but the progenitor, the experimental form, as it were. The termites, invested with more than human intelligence, had formed these underground cities themselves, cities replete with every scientific need and requiring but little of the dying Earth so small were they. Only underground was there safety from the dying atmosphere.

Yes, Nature had been clever in her organization and would be even cleverer when it came to the last mutation into bacteria. Indestructible, bacteria that could live in space, float to other worlds, to begin anew. The eternal cycle.

Carson looked up suddenly, puzzled as to why he should know all these things. At what he beheld he sprang to his feet, only to sit down again as he found his legs were numbed with cold.

There was a small army of ants quite close to him, like a black mat on the smooth red of the ground. Thought transference! That was how he had known. The truth had been forced into his mind deliberately. He realized it clearly now for there came a bombardment of mental questions, but from such a multitude of minds that they failed to make any sense.

'Shelter,' he cried. 'Food and warmth — that is what I want. I have come out of Time — a wanderer — and it was an accident that brought me here. You will regard me as an ancient type, therefore I am surely useful to you. If I stay out here the cold will soon kill me.'

'You created your own accident, Blake Carson,' came one clear wave of thought. 'Had you died as the Time-law proclaimed you would have passed on to the next stage of existence, the stage apart from this one. You chose instead to try and defeat Time in order that you might enact vengeance. We, who understand Time, Space, and Life, see what your intentions were.

'You cannot have help now. It is the law of the cosmos that you must live and die by its dictates. And death such as you will

125

experience this time will not be the normal transition from this plane to another but transition to a plane we cannot even visualize. You have forever warped the cosmic line of Time you were intended to pursue. You can never correct that warp.'

Blake Carson stared, wishing he could shift his icebound limbs. He was dying even now, realized it clearly, but interest kept his mentality still alert.

'Is this hospitality?' he whispered. 'Is this the scientific benevolence of an advanced age? How can you be so pitiless when you know why I sought revenge?'

'We know why, certainly, but it is trivial compared to your infinite transgression in trying to twist scientific law to your own ends. Offence against science is unforgivable, no matter what the motive. You are a throwback, Blake Carson — an outsider! Especially so to us. You never found Hart Cranshaw, the man you wanted. You never will.'

Blake Carson's eyes narrowed suddenly. He noticed that as the thoughts reached him the body of ants had receded quite a distance, evidently giving up interest in him and returning to their domain. But the power of the thoughts reaching him did not diminish.

Abruptly he saw the reason for it. One termite, larger than the others, was alone on the red soil. Carson gazed at it with smouldering eyes, the innermost thoughts of the tiny thing probing his brain.

'I understand,' he whispered. 'Yes, I understand! Your thoughts are being bared to me. You are Hart Cranshaw. You are the Hart Cranshaw of this age. You gained your end. You stole my invention — yes, became the master of science, the lord of the Earth, just as you had planned. You found that there was a way to keep on the normal plane after each death, a way entirely successful if death did not come by electrocution. That was what shattered my plan — the electric chair.

'But you went on and on, dying and being born again with a different and yet identical body. An eternal man, mastering more and more each time!' Carson's voice had risen to a shriek. Then he calmed. 'Until at last Nature changed you

127

into an ant, made you the master of even the termite community. How little did I guess that my discovery would hand you the world. But if I have broken cosmic law, Hart Cranshaw, so have you. You have cheated your normal time action, time and again, with numberless deaths. You have stayed on this plane when you should have moved on to others. Both of us are transgressors. For you, as for me, death this time will mean the unknown.'

A power that was something other than himself gave Blake Carson strength at that moment. Life surged back into his leaden limbs and he staggered to his feet.

'We have come together again, Hart, after all these quintillions of years. Remember what I said long ago? To everything there is an appointed time? Now I know why you don't want to save me.'

He broke off as with sudden and fantastic speed the lone termite sped back towards the mass of his departing colleagues. Once among them, as Carson well knew, there would be no means of identification.

With this realization he forced himself into action and leaped. The movement was the last he could essay. He dropped on his face, and his hand closed round the scurrying insect. It escaped. He watched it run over the back of his hand — then frantically across his palm as he opened his fingers gently.

He had no idea how long he lay watching it — but at last it ran to the tip of his thumb. His first finger closed on his thumb suddenly — and crushed.

He found himself gazing at a black smear on thumb and finger.

He could move his hand no further. Paralysis had gripped his limbs completely. There was a deepening, crushing pain in his heart. Vision grew dim. He felt himself slipping — But with the transition to Beyond he began to realize something else. He had not cheated Time! Neither had Hart Cranshaw! They had done all this before somewhere — would do it again — endlessly, so long as Time itself should exist. Death — transition — rebirth — evolution — back again to the age of the amoeba — upwards to man — the laboratory — the electric chair . . .

Eternal. Immutable!

5

Sweet Mystery of Life

To Idiot Jake the world was peaceful: it was devoid of all worries, tumults and fears. To the intellectuals, Idiot Jake was an object of pity; to the harassed he was a man to be envied. His simple mind did not know the meaning of anxiety.

As long as he could sit on the parapet of the small stone bridge spanning the Bollin Brook he was satisfied. If he had any old paper which he could tear into fragments and toss into the gurgling water below it was to him a close approach to Paradise.

The small English village where he lived with his hard-working widowed mother was serenely sleepy on this autumn Sunday morning. The sunlight gleamed on thatched roofs still damp from departed frosts; smoke curled lazily from crazy little chimneys into a placid blue sky . . .

And on the bridge over the brook Idiot Jake sat in his patched overalls and tattered panama hat. He was long and spare with a narrow face and cramped shoulders. Only in the receding chin and loosely controlled mouth was the evidence of his mental deficiency to be seen. Surprisingly enough, his eyes were very sharp and very blue.

Absently, he looked into the flowing water coursing below him and wished that he had some paper fragments to throw into it. Somehow, though, it was too much of an effort to go and search for them . . .

★　★　★

Half a mile from the village centre, on its outskirts, indeed, and well screened by dense beech trees, stood the home of Harvey Maxted. Nobody in Bollin village knew exactly how Maxted occupied himself. He seemed too young to be a hermit, too thoroughly sane and genial to be an inventor. So tongues wagged, as they always do in a little hamlet perched on the edge of the world

Actually, Maxted was by no means mysterious. He had quite a good Civil Service post in London, to which he travelled back and forth every day. If he chose to live in the quaint old house bequeathed to him by his parents it was entirely his own affair; and if he had decided to live alone except for a fifty-year-old manservant named Belling, that, too, was nobody's business but his own.

He did it for a reason, of course — to have a quiet spot where he could pursue botanical experiments unhindered. Flowers, products of the most brilliant grafting processes, bloomed in every part of the great conservatories attached to the house. Even an old glass-walled, glass-roofed annex, which had once been his artist father's studio had now been converted into a horticulturist's paradise, and apart from the flowers, it also boasted all manner of technical apparatus.

Harvey Maxted, thirty-eight, with plenty of money and a keen investigative brain, had one ambition — to produce that much sought after botanical miracle — a jet black rose.

On this particular Sunday morning he stood before a framed area of soil and fertiliser set directly in the rays of the hot September sun streaming through the glass wall. His young good-looking face was tense with effort. In some odd way his strong, masculine figure seemed out of keeping amidst the exquisite botanical creations looming all around him.

Going down on his knees he went to work steadily in the special area, putting a slender cutting deep in the prepared soil and pressing down with his thumbs all around it. For half an hour he stayed at his task, then, thankful for relief from the intense heat of the window, he left the conservatory and wandered into the house, meditating as he went.

Belling, his servant and confidant, was crossing the hall at the same time.

'Do you think you'll be successful this time, sir?' he enquired, pausing.

Harvey Maxted smiled ruefully. 'All I can say is that I ought to be — but with eighteen failures in trying to produce Erebus, the black rose, I'm losing some of my confidence. In fact, I'm probably crazy to try it anyway. Pride, Belling — that is what it amounts to. I want to feel that I am able to accomplish the impossible!'

'And you will, sir!' the older man declared, nodding his grey head reassuringly. 'You see if you don't.'

'Maybe you're right . . . ' Maxted reflected for a moment, then added: 'I'm going out for an hour or two. See that the conservatory doors are kept locked.'

'You can rely on it, sir.'

* * *

It was late evening when Maxted returned home. He ate a late dinner leisurely, read for an hour, then went into the conservatory annex for a final look at his rose clipping before retiring. But the moment he reached that frame of soil and fertiliser he stopped in dismay.

The cutting had withered completely, lay limp and yellow, with every trace of life drained out of it! For a moment or two Maxted could not believe it — then he twirled round and shouted angrily for

Belling. Within a moment or two the elderly manservant came hurrying in.

'Something the matter, sir?' he asked in surprise.

'I'll say there is! Did you follow out my instructions and keep these doors locked while I was away?'

'But of course I did, sir.' Belling was genuinely distressed. 'I know how valuable everything is in here.'

'You didn't open any of the windows or ventilators from the outside?' Maxted broke off and grinned apologetically, patted the man's arm. 'Sorry, Belling — that was unfair of me. But it's damned strange for that cutting to die like that! It means the end of twelve months' careful grafting . . . '

Belling considered for a moment. 'Perhaps the heat, sir?'

'Not in this case: the heat was an essential part of the experiment . . . ' Maxted leaned over the frame and lifted the dead cutting between finger and thumb. 'Just as though some other plant had claimed the soil and taken the nature out of it,' he muttered. 'In the same way that cultivated plants have a struggle to live near strong trees.'

There was a puzzled silence for a moment or two, then Maxted stood straight again and sighed heavily.

'I simply don't understand it, that's all. I know this soil to be chemically pure . . . I'll have to sleep on the problem, Belling, and when I come home from town tomorrow night I'll take a careful look at this soil.'

All next day as he pursued his normal occupation in the City Maxted could not help himself thinking about his dead rose cutting. Even a keen gardener might have been baffled by the occurrence, but with Harvey Maxted it was something much more. He was a botanical scientist, understanding mysteries of the plant world not even known in the ordinary way . . . Yes, something was decidedly wrong, and nothing else but an analysis of the soil could show what it was.

Maxted wasted no time in getting home that evening and even less time on a meal. Then he unlocked the research conservatory and hurried in, switching on the powerful floodlamps.

The rose cutting had shrivelled now into a mere piece of brown stick, but, in its place something else was showing, just peeping above the rich black soil. Maxted stared at it fixedly. It looked just like the smooth, fleshy head of a toadstool, perhaps an inch across, yet it was more bulbous.

Very cautiously he felt it and, to his amazement, it jerked away slightly from his touch, as though with nervous reflex action.

'What the devil — !' Maxted was dumbfounded for a moment, then he swung round and bawled, 'Belling! Belling — come here!'

Belling came, his tired face troubled. In a moment he assessed the incredulity on Maxted's face.

'Something gone wrong, sir?' he asked anxiously.

'I'll be damned if I know — unless it is that I've worked so long among these plants I've started seeing things — . Take a look at that thing where the rose cutting was. Tell me what you think it is. It — it recoils like the head of a tortoise when you touch it!'

Belling's lined mouth gaped for a moment as he realised the immense implication behind the statement. Then he stretched out a bony finger and tapped the fleshy looking nodule. Again it jerked and the soil around it shifted infinitesimally.

'Great God!' he whispered, his eyes wide. 'It's alive, sir — definitely alive. But what is it?'

'I don't know,' Maxted confessed worriedly. 'I wanted to produce a rare specimen and it looks as though I've done it!'

His first shock over, Belling's maturity came to his aid. Stooping, he looked at the nodule intently in the bright light. Presently he glanced up with the oddest expression.

'I think we should examine this under the microscope, sir,' he said. 'Silly though it may sound, I believe I can see the outline of a — a face!'

'A what!' Maxted exclaimed, startled. 'Hang it all, man — '

138

'The microscope should settle the argument, sir.'

Maxted rubbed the back of his head bemusedly, then he turned and went over to the bench. Bringing back the heavy binocular microscope, he succeeded finally in balancing it so that he could train the lenses directly on the object in the frame.

Wondering vaguely what he would see, he adjusted the eyepieces. Inwardly, he was prepared for the unusual, the fantastic — for anything indeed except the monstrous impossibility of what he did see.

For there was a face!

Belling had spoken the truth, and under the powerful lenses and brilliant light everything was in pin-sharp detail. The rounded nodule had now become a completely hairless head. Underneath it were perfectly chiselled features — a long straight nose, tightly closed lips and round chin. The eyelids were lowered at the moment, giving the face a mask-like aspect of dead serenity.

'Well, sir?'

Belling's eager voice compelled Maxted

to drag his gaze from the fascinating vision. He motioned helplessly to the microscope and Belling peered long and hard. When at last he withdrew his eyes he and Maxted were two men facing the unbelievable.

'A plant — shaped like a human being — growing in soil . . . '

Maxted uttered the words in jerks. 'It's utterly without precedent, either in botany or biology. There has to be a reason for this, Belling, something to make us realise that we are not insane!'

'We can't both be insane, sir.'

'No — I suppose not. This — it. Is it male or female?'

'Can't tell very well, sir . . . yet.'

They looked again at the nodule and it seemed to both of them that there was a constant suggestion of growth about it. It was enlarging even as they watched.

'Belling . . . ' Maxted gripped his servant's arm tightly, his face drawn with the effort of trying to understand. 'Belling, we've stumbled on something infinitely more amazing than a black rose! We've got to watch what happens. Best thing we can do is stay in here and sleep in turns.'

'Yes, sir,' Belling agreed excitedly. 'Indeed yes!'

The decision arrived at, they drew up chairs and then seated themselves where they could watch the enigma in the frame . . . The fact remained that the thing was certainly growing . . . But into *what?*

*   *   *

Maxted and Belling soon discovered that their vigil was not to be a matter of hours, or even of days — but three weeks. During this period the conservatory was kept electrically at the same high temperature as on the morning when the rose cutting had been planted. When he had to be absent, at his Civil Service work in London, Maxted held down his emotions as much as possible — but all the time his thoughts were carrying the remembrance of what he had seen in the conservatory so far.

Then, the moment time permitted, he was rushing homeward again, bolted a meal while Belling related the day's progress; then they went together to survey the miracle's advancement.

The former nodule in the experimental frame had now become an obviously human creature, standing alone in the special bed of soil and surrounded by plants, which screened any chance draught. The sex was definitely female, down to the waist. From this point, however, the trunk of the body branched off into a myriad grey filigrees which, in the fashion of nerves, trailed along and sank into the soil.

A woman, yes — or half a woman — her nakedness concealed by an Oriental dressing gown as a concession to convention. A woman, yes, indescribably, magnetic, with her now opened enormous green eyes and masses of Albino-blonde hair on the formerly bald scalp. A woman who thrived on fertilisers, humanly poisonous material, and crushed bone residue; a woman the pupils of whose eyes contracted and expanded with startling rapidity at the least variation of light.

Mysterious! Incredible!

So far the woman had made no attempt to communicate. In fact, no sound whatever had escaped her. She seemed able to take nourishment either by the mouth or through the weird mass of sensory nerves trailing from her like roots. At other times her eyes were closed and her body relaxed as though she were sleeping.

'Have you any theories, sir, as to what happened to cause this?' Belling asked when they had finished their latest survey.

'One — just one,' Maxted breathed. 'It can explain it, but it is so incredible I hardly believe it myself . . . Do you know Arrhenius' theory?'

Belling reflected. He had a good smattering of general knowledge.

'You mean the one about him believing that life came to Earth through indestructible spores surviving the void of space and then germinating here?'

'That's the one . . . ' Maxted mopped his streaming face and glanced at the thermometer. It stood at 120°F. 'It may be possible,' he went on, 'that somehow a wandering spore was in the soil when I planted that rose cutting. The cutting died because of the strength of the germinating spore drawing all the nature out of the soil. In this conservatory here we must have accidentally reproduced all the conditions necessary to germinate the spore . . .'

Maxted looked at the silent woman-plant long and earnestly as she slept, head drooping on her breast.

'Yes, I'm sure I'm right,' he resumed. 'Life on any other world would be vastly different from ours. This half-woman must belong to a world where intelligent life takes on the form of a plant. A hot, burning world — Where, Belling? What miracle have we come upon?'

To this there was no immediate answer. Both men kept unceasing watch on the astounding creation in the nights and days that followed . . .

* * *

She grew no taller, but there was greater development in the shoulders as time passed. Once even she seemed ill and wilting, but a saturation of the soil with water and phosphates revived her.

During this period she remained practically motionless, her eyes studying the conservatory intently — or else the two men as they surveyed her. It was as though she were trying to determine the nature of her surroundings. When she moved at all it comprised a sinuous writhing of her well-rounded arms, as though she yearned to stretch herself . . .

Then one morning, when the autumn sun was streaming through the great windows, she made the first sound. It began at about the pitch of a soprano's high C and then sailed up effortlessly through two octaves in the purest bell-like clearness it had ever been Belling's good luck to hear. Immediately he rushed out for Maxted, who was sleeping after his night's watch.

'She's singing, sir.' Belling shouted, as he blundered into the bedroom.

Maxted listened drowsily to the silver purity of those notes, then he hurried out of bed and dragged on some clothes . . . The astounding woman was singing with the joyous abandon of a nightingale when they burst in upon her. In fact, their entry was perhaps too sudden, for she stopped abruptly.

'Shut the door!' Maxted ordered. 'We can't risk any cold air in here . . . '

He went over to the woman slowly, stared into her huge green eyes. The pupils, so abysmally wide in artificial light, were now contracted to pin points in the glare of sunshine, leaving great emerald-coloured irises.

'Who are you?' Maxted asked in an awed voice, repeating a question he had asked dozens of times already. 'How did you ever get here?'

The eyes, like those of a tigress, stared back at him hypnotically. He realised that such delicately constructed orbs were intended for a planet of alternate glare and total dark . . . Blinding sun for a very long day; perhaps moonless night for a like period. A world of titanic vegetation perhaps — of such people as this . . . ?

Maxted gave himself a little shake and turned his gaze away by sheer physical effort. Belling was beside him, watching and wondering.

'Have you — a language?' Belling asked urgently.

The woman gestured with two copper-coloured arms, and somehow it revealed that she did not understand. Then from her cherry red mouth, with its oddly pointed teeth, came a stream of sing-song notes in that breathtaking purity of tone.

'Speech, sir!' Belling insisted urgently, clutching Maxted's arm. 'That's what it is. She's trying to talk to us.'

'Yes . . . ' Maxted listened to her in bewildered attention. 'Yes — speech.'

Even so it was but the commencement of weeks of hard work to come, of the exchange of words. But gradually the woman seemed to understand what was meant. By means of pantomime and untiring patience, Maxted struggled to bridge the gap between species. In the intervals between these spells of study the woman either sang gloriously or slept.

Those times when he had to be away on business were the hardest for Maxted, but somehow he got through it.

★　★　★

Inevitably, though, the conservatory's secret did not remain within those hot glass walls. Seated on the bridge parapet one morning, tearing up a piece of paper and watching the strips flutter into the brook below, was Idiot Jake. He heard a voice of uncommon range and clarity floating from somewhere beyond the village, born on the south wind.

Its beauteous harmony attracted him, drew him irresistibly

He traced it finally to the conservatory, where a slightly open ventilator permitted the sound to come forth. Idiot Jake could see quite clearly through the plain glass windows — and he started a rumour, which went through the clannish, scandal-loving community of the village with seven league boots.

Harvey Maxted, the mystery man, the apparent misogamist, had got an ash-blonde woman living with him! Been no announcement of a marriage or anything, either! Jake himself had seen her, both in the day and at night. She always sat in that little outbuilt conservatory, singing or talking and dressed in a sort of Oriental costume.

That she was only half a woman was not apparent to the prying busybodies of Bollin. The shrubs surrounding the special soil bed hid the filigree of nervous tendrils that began at the waistline. From outside it looked as though she were sitting down among the plants.

In groups, by night, the denizens of the village crept into the grounds of the house and looked through the unscreened windows on to the scene within. They said it was not even decent and that Maxted ought to be locked up for it, and his servant with him . . . Then, gradually, they tired of their scandal and ceased to bother.

All except Idiot Jake. Though he no longer risked detection by hiding in the grounds in the daylight, he was certainly there every night, his crafty pale blue eyes watching over the thick bushes, his warped brain considering all manner of speculations about the terribly lovely woman who either sat and gestured or else sang with a richness which stirred Idiot Jake to the depths.

Maxted and Belling, absorbed in their

efforts to communicate with the plant-woman, never even gave eavesdropping a thought. That the conservatory had no window shades they knew full well, but since it and the house were in the midst of grounds the possibility of being overlooked never occurred to them.

Besides, they were making good progress in language exchange now. The woman was able to express herself with comparative fluency, and where she stumbled the gap could always be filled in. Certainly the time had come, in Maxted's opinion, for a determined effort to solve the mystery.

'Just who are you?' he asked the woman, seated on one side of the soil bed and Belling on the other.

'I come from the moon of another planet,' the woman's dulcet voice replied, and she added an arm gesticulation.

'Moon of the another planet?' Maxted repeated, frowning. 'You mean outside of the solar system?'

'Another solar system,' the woman agreed, then she hesitated as she chose her words. Slowly, with many pauses, she began to tell her story. 'My name is Cia. I lived, ages ago, upon the satellite of another world. Upon this satellite, as upon the parent world, there existed — and still does on the parent world — a race of beings like me. I am not either male or female, as you would call it, but both . . . '

'You mean hermaphrodite?' Maxted asked sharply.

'If you call two sexes in one that — yes. Many of your Earth plants have that quality and some of your animals and birds. New plants — new living beings in our case — are born simply by the casting of seed. Under the influence of rich soil it grows and can choose its own sex as far as appearance is concerned. Nature has cursed our race by making us plantlike and immobile;, but as a compensation she has given us vast intelligence. Even the ability to read thoughts: that is how I have learned your language so quickly. Whether it be a jest of Nature to give great intellect to beings who cannot move from the spot where they are born, I do not know . . . '

Maxted looked sharply at the absorbed Belling across the soil bed, then the woman resumed haltingly.

'This, though, I do know. Life — our life — became so profuse on our moon, and the myriad roots became so deep and destructive, that it finally smashed the satellite in pieces, just like some of your climbing plants tear down a wall. We were aware in advance of what was happening and so contracted ourselves back into spore form — '

'How could that be done?' Belling asked.

'I've heard of certain plants, and even animals, which can contract themselves,' Maxted answered. 'Take, for instance, certain sea squirts which spend the winter in the form of small white masses in which the organs of the normal animal are quite absent. In the spring they reverse the process and grow up again. Sea anemones do the same thing if starved of nutriment. So do flat worms. But usually this contraction business applies only to the invertebrates. You, Cia, appear to have a backbone.'

'Not in the sense you know it,' she answered. 'It is hard tissue, not solid bone.'

'That would explain your ability to

shrink then,' Maxted admitted. 'As for your male-female unity, we call it parthenogenesis.'

'This power to contract does not destroy our intelligence,' the woman resumed, 'because in a sense we are still alive. When the satellite broke up we were, of course, cast adrift into space. Myriads of us must have drifted down on to the parent world; drawn by the gravity, to take root and flourish anew. In my case, I can only think that cosmic tides wafted me across the infinite to this world where I have lain, in a form of suspended animation, for untold ages. Then you produced conditions here identical to those on my former world and I came to life. My effort to understand explains why I took time to communicate. Our ability to what you call 'sing' comes from the need of calling to each other over great distances . . . '

There was a silence and Maxted drew a deep breath. He looked at the woman from a far off world, and then at Belling; but before he could speak his attention was caught by something outside one of the huge windows.

A face was looking into the conservatory — a thin, fox-like face topped by a battered panama hat. The licentious blue eyes of Idiot Jake were watching every detail.

'By God!' Maxted breathed angrily, jumping up. 'I'll show him. It's that damned yokel out of the village — '

He strode to the door and opened it, closing it quickly again to prevent any drastic change of air. In a few quick strides he was out through the back entrance into the grounds. Evidently Idiot Jake had guessed what was intended, for he had just commenced to slink away into the bushes. In one dive Maxted was upon him, whirling him round with a tight grip on the collar of his shabby coat.

'Just a minute, Jake! What are you doing here?'

'Nothin' mister . . . ' Jake cringed and averted his face. 'I just wanted to see the pretty singer . . .You can't hit me for that!'

Maxted tightened his lips for a moment.

'The pretty singer, eh? Is that what you have been telling everybody in the village?

How often have you been here?'

'Never before,' Jake lied emphatically, and Maxted gave him a shove.

'All right — you get back home before I break your neck. And if I ever find you on my property again I'll hand you over to the police. Go on — get moving!'

Jake touched the brim of his battered panama and grinned vacantly, then he went loping off amidst the bushes.

Maxted came back into the conservatory with a troubled frown.

'I don't like it,' he confessed to Belling when he had briefly recounted what had happened. 'That imbecile is likely to spread all kinds of idiotic tales — granting even that he hasn't done so already.'

'Doesn't seem to be much we can do, sir,' Belling reflected. 'The damage, if any, is done already.'

Maxted nodded regretfully, then, with a shrug, which seemed to indicate that he had decided to drop the matter he turned to look again at Cia. She was watching him intently.

'This meeting between Earth and another planet — or at any rate that planet's moon — is about the most marvellous thing that ever happened,' he said. 'But wonderful though it is, it is incomplete in itself. We are just individuals representing our respective species. There will have to be a way found for space to be bridged and our two worlds to have exchange of visits . . . You understand what I mean, Cia?'

'I understand,' she assented.

'Good! Tell me, with all the high intelligence your race possesses, have you any ideas on interstellar travel?'

'Yes, although much is theory. Being immobile we have no use for space travel, but handed down in the knowledge of our race is the story of a ship from space that crashed upon our world. From the few survivors — they were somewhat similar to your race, and our climate suited them — we learned much about the construction and working of their machine.'

Maxted stroked his chin and frowned.

'Strange that Earth has never had visitors from another planet. I wonder — could these visitors of yours have come from our system — Mars perhaps?'

'No. According to our knowledge, they came from the outer deeps of space, and only chance directed them to us. Most of the travellers were killed when the ship crashed — the few survivors were unable to repair the damage and spent the rest of their lives living amongst us. Their knowledge expanded our concepts tremendously.'

There was silence for a while, whilst Maxted paced slowly up and down the conservatory; then Cia resumed.

'We of my world need a race like yours to free us from bondage. We are intellectual giants chained down by Nature. None of our mighty ideas can bear fruit until we have somebody with us who can move about and so help us. I am prepared to give you the secrets of spaceship design and atomic power, which you will need for propulsion — if you in turn will pledge yourselves to work side by side with us to free us from enslavement.'

Maxted was silent, overawed by the immensity of the proposition. He reflected for quite a time, watched anxiously by Belling and the woman, before he made up his mind.

'I cannot, of course, speak for my entire race, Cia; it would take years to make everybody understand what is happening here, and even then there would be no guarantee of others agreeing with my viewpoint that we should help you and your people. But, speaking for myself and the many scientists who for years have been crying out for a chance like this, I am willing to co-operate. Once the thing is done collusion between our worlds is inevitable.'

'Very well,' the woman said. 'I realize that you cannot convince your race without proof, so I shall make the secrets your property.'

'Now?' Maxted questioned eagerly.

'No, tomorrow night. I must have time to consider the relative differences between your mathematics and mine. For tonight I prefer to be left alone.'

'All right,' Maxted assented. 'But one or other of us will remain on guard outside. I don't feel any too happy after that village idiot has been prowling about . . .'

★ ★ ★

Contrary to Maxted's fears, however, Idiot Jake did not present himself again during the night, or during the next day — Sunday. And by the time evening came both men were too absorbed in the alien plant-woman's slow explanation of profound secrets to give any thought to Idiot Jake.

For two hours Cia talked and gave mathematical formulae, which Maxted wrote down laboriously in his notebook. In that two hours he learned, through figures anyway, the secrets of new metals and the many different essentials necessary in a ship designed to cross interstellar space. He learned how atomic force could be extracted and controlled with complete safety and the calculations necessary for the trajectory across space to Cia's solar system. These and many more Cia gave him, until his head began to ache with the thoughts being instilled inside it.

Yes, upon those sheets of paper, which Maxted finally set aside on the bench

159

were secrets which could lay the foundations of an interstellar empire.

Then, suddenly, just as the long effort to understand each other was over, there was a violent explosive crack from one of the windows. A heavy piece of tree branch came hurtling inwards in a shower of glass.

'What the devil!' Maxted swung round angrily and for a moment there was a vision of Idiot Jake's vindictively grinning face. Then he dashed out of sight and vanished in the darkness of the grounds.

Maxted took three swift strides towards the shattered window, only to pause as Cia gave a desperate, despairing cry and Belling shouted in horror.

Something was happening to the plant-woman. Her head was drooping, her face suffused with an expression of indescribable anguish. Her soft copper-tinted flesh was turning grey and forming into dry and dusty scales.

'It's the cold, sir!' Belling shouted, seizing Maxted's arm. 'It's killing her! The temperature's gone down — '

Maxted made a slow, stupid movement,

unable to decide what he ought to do. In any case, it was too late now. The night air streaming into the conservatory was charged with frost and under its withering breath the strange being of a superheated world wilted until she looked as if she had been soaked in liquid air. She began to take on a brittle, crystallised aspect.

'Cia!' Maxted gasped, clutching her hand, then he stared in horror as it snapped off in his grip like a rotten branch.

'She's dead, sir,' Belling whispered, white-faced. 'She's as brittle as a carrot!'

He paused and both he and Maxted swung round as a police officer came striding in through the shattered window, followed by a surging mass of the village populace and — in the background — the drooling Idiot Jake.

'Now, sir!' Police Constable Adams looked round the conservatory curiously, then at the frozen grey image that had been a woman. 'Now, sir, what's all this 'ere about you 'aving a woman in 'ere? Always sat in the same place? I've heard all about it.'

'From that idiot, Jake, eh?' Maxted asked bitterly. 'Or from these villagers?' and he looked sourly at them as they formed in a curious semi-circle.

'I 'eard of a woman being ill-treated in 'ere, sir,' P.C. Adams said. 'I considered it my duty to h'investigate.'

'Sheer imagination, constable, on the part of Jake,' Maxted said, trying hard to keep his temper. 'I found him on my property last night and kicked him out. Tonight he smashes a window for revenge and spreads a trumped-up tale. And you've no authority to break in on me like this, either!'

'Sorry, sir.' Adams began to look uncomfortable. 'I just thought I'd better — '

'We all saw that woman!' one of the villagers piped up. 'An' we heard her voice, too. She were a fine singer, she were.'

Maxted gave a weary smile.

'The voice, let me assure you, was from an instrument I am working upon. As for the woman — well, can't a man fashion a statue to place among his flowers? Look for yourselves!'

He pointed to the dead, granite-like

162

Cia. P.C. Adams looked at her, touched her hard shoulders, brooded over the solidly frozen tendrils in the soil as though he wondered what they were — then he put his notebook away and touched his helmet.

'Sorry, sir; been a mistake somewhere. I'll say goodnight. Outside, you people! Outside!'

When at last they had all gone Maxted relaxed and rubbed his forehead.

'We might have got in a nasty mess, Belling. We never thought of conventions . . . Poor Cia! Obviously she froze to death before she had a chance to adapt herself into spore form or protect herself against the cold. Damn Idiot Jake! Damn him!'

'At least we have the secrets, sir,' Belling said. 'Over on the bench there is our passport to another — '

He stopped dead. Maxted caught his look of consternation and gazed as well. There was no sign of papers or notebook anywhere.

★ ★ ★

The following morning it was calm and sunny. Two distracted men had searched all night and failed to find the secrets that could link two worlds.

On the bridge over the Bollin Brook Idiot Jake sat and hummed to himself, a bundle of papers in each tattered pocket. As he watched the torn strips flutter down and float away the world seemed to him to be laughing. Perhaps it was — ironically.

6

Chewing Gum Murder

No one in our village was more happy, more placid, more level-headed, and more in love with life than my Uncle Neb. His cheeks were always aglow and his gait ever springy, and he had a cheery greeting for everyone — man, woman, or child. If ever a being loved every moment of his existence it was my Uncle, Nebuchadnezzar Chigley. The only time I ever saw a frown cross his face was when anyone — just to tease him — addressed him by the full flavour of his name. He was regarded as one of the permanent features of Duckswater Village — as much a part of the place as the Norman church, or the ancient stocks, or the annual flower show.

So, when one bright summer's morning, I paid one of my frequent visits to Uncle Neb's trim cottage where he lived alone, I was worried to find his bottle of milk still standing on the doorstep and his morning newspaper still sticking out of the letterbox. I was worried, because Uncle Neb was an early riser and it was now ten o'clock with the sun already well up.

Nervously I went back to my own cottage and got the spare key which Uncle Neb had long entrusted to me so that I could put his grocery and things inside when he happened to be out for the day. On these occasions he always let me know beforehand: and that was why I was worried.

Tremblingly, I turned the key in the lock and stepped into the little sitting room, which opened directly from the street. The lay Uncle Neb, quite, quite dead with a gaping hole in his head and a heavy pistol gripped in his right hand. I was completely horrified, but I did not lose my head. I knelt and touched his forehead just to make sure; it was icy cold. Poor Uncle Neb. Dead by his own hand. The last person in the world one would have thought would have taken his own life.

I called the police, who searched for motives. Uncle Neb had left no letter; evidently his act was quite unpremeditated. Plainly, he had just had his evening meal when he had come back to the sudden determination to end his life. A book lay open on the arm of his favourite chair; it had no bearing on the tragedy, for it was *The Pickwick Papers* — a jolly, cheerful, laughter-inducing book if ever there was one. Nobody reading it should ever feel despondent. Some sudden brainstorm had evidently come upon poor Uncle Neb.

Then there was the revolver, I never knew him to possess such a thing. He had a few old flint-lock pistols and such-like hanging on the walls of his sitting room, but their purpose was decorative, like the Staffordshire china cottages on the mantelpieces, the stuffed fish which were reminders of his angling days, and the full-rigged sailing ships in bottles which were a hobby of his, and with which he delighted to amuse and mystify my children, his great grand-nieces and nephews.

No doubt he had bought the revolver

for the purpose of self-defence, although I had never known him to show any sign of nervousness at living alone. He was, although in his sixties, a man of splendid physique, and with his knowledge of holds, gained during his service as a master-at-arms in the Royal Navy, he was more than a match for any small-time crook who might have broken into his cottage. I just couldn't understand that revolver. Maybe it was one of those war souvenirs, and that Uncle Neb bought it off some returned soldier who had pitched him a hard luck tale. Uncle Neb would buy almost anything; his cottage was full of all sorts of knick-knacks that he had that he had picked up in his travels in various parts of the world. He used to point to little bits of china, for example, that stood on the mantelpiece, and chuckle to himself as he told me how much they were worth.

'That's a bit of *famille vert*, Moira,' he would say. 'I picked it up in Peking way back in nineteen-five. Worth a lot o'money, that is. One like that was sold at Christie's the other day for a thousand quid; and your old Uncle Neb bought that for less than a thousand pennies.' I used to laugh, for I looked upon his estimates of the values of his funny little bits of china as just sailor's yarns.

'When I shuffle off, Moira my girl, it's all yours. It'll help you educate the children — and there's nothing like in these days of hard competition. Why, if I'd only had an education I'd have been an Admiral instead of just a petty officer.'

I believe he would have, too, for after he left the navy he spent most of his time reading — not in made-up yarns but history and travel books and heavy stuff like that. He would even read his dictionary right through, and I don't believe there was a word in that dictionary he couldn't spell, In the old days they used to have spelling-bees in our village, and he would win the first prize every time — even against people like the vicar and the doctor and the local lawyer. Finally they barred him from the spelling-bees because nobody else would compete when the result was a forgone conclusion.

It was hard to believe that he had gone: harder still to credit that he had taken his own life. Hardest of all to believe, however, was the fact that instead of leaving his property to me he had left it all to a nephew in America whom none of us had seen for over ten years. He was the son of another brother of Uncle Neb's, and I had never heard Uncle Neb say a good word about him. Not that he said any bad ones; that wasn't Uncle Neb's way, but for a nephew to whom you intend to leave all your property, my cousin Japhet — or Jafe, as he was called for short, was very seldom spoken about by Uncle Neb. I think that was really because Jafe — who seemed to have lived in just about every state in America — never wrote unless he wanted something.

Latterly, of course, it had become difficult for Uncle Neb to respond to these hard-luck stories because of government currency regulations, but in the old days Jafe used to soak his uncle good and proper. When Neb could no longer come across with the cash, Jafe stopped writing those affectionate letters, and in fact I don't think Uncle Neb had heard from him for four or five years before he died.

However, there it was. When the police were rummaging around Uncle Neb's house for clues to the tragedy they had come across the will — all properly drawn up, witnessed and stamped as required by law. The police asked me if I knew the name and address of Uncle Neb's solicitor. I could only think of Mr. Vellam, the lawyer who used to compete with Uncle Neb at the spelling bees, and with whom he was quite friendly. It turned out that Mr. Vellam had acted for Uncle Neb in various matters, including, he told me, a previous will that Uncle Neb had made.

'I am terribly sorry to hear that you are receiving no benefit from your Uncle's will, Mrs. Brenton,' sympathized Mr. Vellam when I met him in the street one day. 'I know he thought the world of you and your children, and to my knowledge it was always his intention that you should benefit; but now there is this other will, executed, apparently, a year ago, leaving everything to this good-for-nothing cousin of yours.

'I really don't understand it. Your Uncle was a friend of mine and I saw no indication at all that he was not in his right mind. Yet this n'er-do-well bird of passage in America inherits the sum of nine thousand pounds. Although it has gone very much against the grain, Mrs. Brenton, I have in my professional capacity been obliged to acquaint him of his — er, h'm — remarkable good fortune, and he has cabled back that he will be over to deal with the matter, by the first available plane in ten days' time.'

* * *

My cousin Japhet arrived as promised. To look at him, he wasn't the sort of person to keep any promise, but then there was nine thousand pounds dangling on the end of this one. He had developed into a tough-looking guy with slits for eyes so that you couldn't tell what, if anything, he was thinking; and a jutting chunk of blue marble for a chin, His whole manner and get-up suggested that at any moment he would produce a gold brick from his pocket.

At his first interview with Mr. Vellam, Jafe wept crocodile tears, saying that he loved his Uncle Neb very dearly and that no amount of money could compensate for his loss, but when Mr. Vellam tactfully suggested to him that he might like to share the proceeds of the estate with me — who had three children to bring up and educate on the little money the State allowed to widows — Jafe would have none of it, even though on his own admission he was well off even by American standards, with many thousands of dollars invested in what he called real estate.

'Bein' sentimental don't get yer nowheres, Mr. Attorney,' he said to Mr. Vellam. 'Why, ef I'da bin sentimental I'da bin jest a hobo ridin' the rods, 'stead of an ace drummer runnin' his own Cadillac an' livin' Ritzy. I like the big money, Mr. Attorney, an' I guess my uncle decided he'd leave his cash to somebody who knew

173

how to spend it, 'stead o' somebody like Mrs. Brenton who's never known what High Livin' is. No, sorry, Mr. Vellam, I'm a business man, not a philanthropist.'

'He's a hard man, Mrs. Brenton, and I doubt whether he is as highly respected in the U.S.A. as he makes himself out to be.' Thus Mr. Vellam unburdened himself to me when he told me, with many shakes of the head, of his unsuccessful efforts to persuade cousin Jafe to be generous to his own kith and kin. 'Still, Mrs. Brenton, you can rely on my doing all I can for you and your children. That much I owe to the memory of my dear friend, your Uncle Neb.'

'It's very kind of you, Mr. Vellam, to say that, but I don't see what else you can do,' I said. 'The will is in perfect order, apparently, and there is no question but that my uncle was in his right mind when he made it. And there could hardly have been any undue influence on Jafe's part, seeing that he was all those thousands of miles away for the past ten years. There it is, all written out in Uncle Neb's own hand and properly witnessed. It's all very queer, Mr. Vellam, but it can't be helped.'

There was a faraway look in Mr. Vellam's eyes as he answered. 'It is, as you say, Mrs. Brenton, very queer, and it may be that I can find an explanation, but at the moment I can say no more.'

* * *

The weeks passed by and I was beginning to recover from the shock of my uncle's death when Mr. Vellam stopped to speak to me in the High Street.

'Don't think I have forgotten that little matter of your uncle's will, Mrs. Brenton,' he said. 'I may have some good news for you soon.' I could not even guess what that news might be, and Mr. Vellam was still uncommunicative.

A week later, however, there came the astonishing news — which I first read in a headline splashed right across the front page of an evening newspaper — that Japhet Stagg a commercial traveller, of Akron, Ohio, had been arrested on suspicion of being concerned in the murder of his uncle, Mr. Nebuchadnezzar Chigley, of Duckswater, Loamshire, England.

I hastened round to Mr. Vellam's office, and his eyes were twinkling brightly as he greeted me in his room with its rows of leather-bound law books ranged round the walls,

'Yes, things are moving, Mrs. Brenton. Of course, no one can be convicted of murder in this country until twelve good men and true have unanimously decided that he is guilty. I gather from communications that have passed between their police and ours, that there will be no fuss about extradition as he has never taken out naturalisation papers and remains a British subject.'

'But I still don't understand, Mr. Vellam what evidence there can be to connect Japhet Stagg with my uncle's death,' I said, 'After all, Jafe was in America and you can hardly commit murder by remote control.'

Mr. Vellam smiled his gentle smile as he answered, 'I'm afraid I cannot say anything about that at the moment. Mrs. Brenton. You see, the course is *sub judice* — that is, it is under consideration by the law, and one cannot do or say anything that might impede the course of justice, my dear. But I think I can safely say that before very long Mr. Japhet Stagg will be standing in the dock at the Central Criminal Court, and that one of the prosecution's witnesses will be myself.'

'But surely, Mr. Vellam, you know nothing about — '

'Have patience, my dear,' he answered. 'In good time you will know as much as I do. Of course, Japhet is doing all he can to avoid being extradited. He's as cunning as a fox. I see that he's just been interviewed in the local lock-up by some newspaper men. He feels quite proud of being in the limelight and mixed up in a very special case. Had it been an American murder nobody would have taken any notice, but as he's suspected of having murdered someone in England — where murders only happen about once a month instead of once a minute — Mr. Japhet Stagg is front-page news. He boasts that he's looking forward to a free trip at the British Government's expense if he *has* to go, and that he'll be suing us for damages for wrongful imprisonment afterwards. He's already negotiating, he says, to sell the newspaper rights in the story in the story of his trial and acquittal, and no doubt Hollywood will be interested too.

'The nine thousand pounds he has inherited from your uncle is just chicken-feed, he says; certainly not enough, as he puts it, to justify a respectable guy like himself bumping off a grand guy like your uncle. He has briefed the best lawyer in Akron to oppose his extradition, so it may be some time before we are able to get him over for trial.'

★ ★ ★

Jafe's lawyer put up a skilful fight for his client. He argued that the evidence against him was purely circumstantial, and that there were no grounds whatever for connecting him with the crime. He submitted definite proof, in the shape of Japhet's passport, to show that he had never been further afield than Canada and Mexico during the whole of his stay in the United States, until the day when he flew to England to collect his inheritance — and by then, as everybody knew, his poor Uncle Neb was already dead.

The lawyer then called two of Japhet's friends to testify that they had been on holiday in Vermont with Jafe at the time when Uncle Neb died. Not that such evidence was necessary, in his opinion; it was enough to show the evidence of Jafe's passport. Whenever one entered a country the passport was stamped with the date and place of entry. Passports could, of course, be tampered with, but he defied anybody to say that this one had been.

When next I saw Mr. Vellam he was looking pretty glum.

'I'm pretty much afraid that unless we can obtain just one more piece of evidence, Mrs. Brenton, that unspeakable Japhet is going to — er — get away with it, as they say over there. American law may seem silly to us, but you can't charge a man with murder when his passport showed he couldn't have been there — even when all sorts of other things point to the fact that he was. I'm very much afraid they are going to release him in a day or two. There's something I feel I can do to prevent that calamity. I'm going to fly over to Akron. Mrs. Brenton; I am doing it out of respect for the memory of a dear old friend, and because I am convinced that my theory that Japhet Stagg murdered your Uncle Neb is right.'

Only a few days had passed before I found that Mr. Vellam's faith in his theory was justified. The application by Scotland Yard for an extradition order had been granted and soon cousin Japhet would be arriving in this country in the custody of British police officers. The accounts in the British newspapers were naturally brief; they would wait until the trial before they spread themselves. But the American papers that Mr. Vellam sent over to me were not so coy.

BRITISH OLD-TIME LAWYER FINDS
MURDER EVIDENCE WHERE
SLEUTHS FAIL

STAGG TO STAND TRIAL IN LONDON

Headlines like this, as big as a shop sign, were splashed all over the leading journals.

⋆ ⋆ ⋆

Mr. Vellam himself returned a day or two later than the papers. When I met him he was much more like his old, cheerful self.

'I found what I was looking for, my dear,' he said, 'as you will have gathered from the papers I sent you. Naturally they were not giving away the whole story. That would only spoil the public interest in the trial when it comes on. 'Keep 'em guessing; keep 'em on tenterhooks' — that seems to be the policy until they can really 'go to town' on the story. But I can tell you this, my dear; I was looking for a photograph. I looked in every photographer's shop in Akron, Ohio; looked not only in their windows but through their stock of negatives inside.

'I was looking for a portrait of somebody; of Japhet Stagg, to be precise, And if you've ever looked through thousands of photographic negatives for

181

the picture of somebody you don't know very well, you'll understand the sort of job I had taken on — especially as I couldn't be certain whether the photograph I sought was to be found in Akron, Ohio, or not. Naturally, during my search through all those negatives with their black faces and white eyes and hair I had to have some idea of what Japhet would look like if his colouring were turned 'inside out', so to speak.

'That was too much to expect without having something as a guide. So I asked the local police office if they had any pictures of Japhet. They had — plenty; they had taken him in every conceivable position, Side, front, and rear elevations and every angle in between. I chose a full-faced, head-and-shoulders picture and asked them if they would do me a negative print from it. The police photographer goggled a bit at this and asked me why I wanted a picture of Stagg all blacked up. I just grinned, and said I much preferred him that way.

Armed with this negative print, I had something to work with, Although I couldn't tell the photographers just whom I was looking for, they spotted my English accent and at once linked my search with the Stagg murder case.

'' 'I don't remember the guy, mister', they all said with a shake of the head. 'Anyway, the name Stagg fails to ring any bell. We get dozens o' folks in here every day for passport photographs. No, we don't keep any prints, but we hold the negatives for a while in case they want any copies to give to their friends. But why would anyone want copies of a passport photo?' They all managed to crack that particular joke, but none of them had any objection to my looking through their stock.

All the same, I had come to the very last photographer in the city before I had any luck — and believe me, in an American city of 300,000 inhabitants there are plenty of photographers. 'I'd like a print of this one in half an hour,' I said to the photographer, 'if you can manage it?' He retired behind a door. There was a faint whirring sound, and he returned with the print in less time than it takes to tell. It was Japhet Stagg all right, but I felt that they could not have convicted him of murder on the strength of that one photograph alone — it was such a shocker. The photographer was a mechanical sort of chap for he had written on the edge of the negative not only the serial number, but the date on which the picture was taken.

'Armed with this information I dashed off to the local passport office. Fortunately, they kept duplicate prints of passport pictures just as we do in England, and as I was able to give the date they were soon able to produce it. They were also able to tell me the name of the holder of the passport to which it was attached, and it was not Japhet Stagg. So that, my dear, is how this matter stands at the moment. I'll see you at the Old Bailey.'

★   ★   ★

When Japhet came up for trial he was remarkably jaunty for a man on trial for his life. He thought he had committed the perfect crime; there were no fingerprints on the revolver with which Uncle Neb had been shot; of that he was certain, for he had worn a pair of rubber gloves. The will itself, which he had forged, was a perfect work of art, which no one would have suspected of being a forgery, but he had made just a tiny mistake that had caught the observant eye of Mr. Vellam. As for his beautiful alibi, that went by the board, for he had flown to this country on a false passport on the very day Uncle Neb had died!

So when prosecuting counsel, opening the case for the Crown, related these facts, it seemed that there was a pretty damning volume of evidence against Japhet. Yet, strangely enough, this would probably have been insufficient under British law to secure a conviction. The forgery of the will had been discovered not by the police but by Mr. Vellam. Familiar as he was with Uncle Neb's writing, even he had been deceived until he noticed that the word 'traveller' was spelt in the American way. With only one '1' — a 'crime' of which Uncle Neb, who was so proud of his spelling, would never have been guilty. Mr. Vellam had the will examined by a handwriting expert, who compared it with some genuine examples of Uncle Neb's handwriting. He found a number of discrepancies which the ordinary person might not have noticed — and he also found the letters which did not tally with Uncle Neb's genuine handwriting were exactly like the same letters in specimens of Japhet's writing with which he had been provided! Enlarged photographs showing these differences and resemblances were handed up for the jury's inspection.

Of course, all this evidence was purely circumstantial; it might prove that he was guilty of forgery, and that he was in England on the very night his uncle died; but where was the proof that he had visited Uncle Neb's cottage on the night of the 15th July? Once again the gentle, quiet little Mr. Vellam supplied the answer. The police had ransacked the cottage for clues and found no sign of any fingerprints other than Uncle Neb's own.

Mr. Vellam, returning from America with the evidence of forgery in his pocket, was not satisfied. Mere forgery, he felt, would never convict Japhet of murder; what he was looking for were some nice fingerprints. Failing some, just one would do! Equipping himself with a pair of rubber gloves, an enormous magnifying glass, and a supercilious detective-constable, he proceeded to the cottage, He thought the magnifying glass might not be necessary, but he had brought it just in case — and the detective-constable was merely there to confirm Mr. Vellam's discoveries, if any. So, donning the gloves, he proceeded to put his theory to the test.

He recalled that the American papers had made frequent references to the fact that Japhet was an inveterate gum-chewer, and that he did not masticate any one piece of gum for long. As soon as the flavour had weakened he would discard his gum and take a fresh piece. In fact, remarked the reporters, he had created a prison record for the amount of gum consumed, and his cell walls were dotted all over with discarded buts of gum.

Obviously, Mr. Vellam told himself, Jafe's gum-chewing indicated a state of tension, and it was highly probable that when he killed Uncle Neb his jaws were working overtime. If so, there might be in the cottage the very piece of evidence that would send Jafe Stagg to the gallows.

'Everything's been gone over with a — er — small-toothcomb,' remarked Detective-Constable Snooty, as Mr. Vellam proceeded to peer into every nook and cranny at the cottage. Mr. Vellam made no reply but proceeded with his search.

At last, exploring with his gloved fingers under the top of the sitting room table, he felt a small, flattish protuberance in the angle formed by one of the table legs and the top.

'Help me turn this table over, will you?' he said to the police officer. The latter gave vent to a very audible professional sniff as he did as he was bidden.

'Just as I suspected — chewing gum!' said Mr. Vellam as the small protuberance was revealed to the light of day.

'Chewing gum?' echoed Detective-Constable Snooty.

'Yes, young man — and don't touch it on any account — it's a pretty lethal piece of gum, I think. Better get one of your police vans round here right away. If I'm not mistaken, that table and its chewing gum is going to be Exhibit A in the case of the trial of Japhet Stagg.'

The table and its piece of gum — after a comparison with the file of fingerprints at Scotland Yard — became, as Mr. Vellam had foretold, Exhibit A at the trial of Japhet Stagg. As Mr. Vellam had foretold, the piece of gum proved to be 'pretty lethal', so lethal, in fact, that it did more than anything else to cause the black cap to be placed upon the judge's head and the rope around Japhet's neck.

He had contrived the 'perfect murder' but for one tiny error; he removed his glove for a moment when he parked his gum under the top of Uncle Neb's sitting room table.

★   ★   ★

'All that remains for me to do now, my dear,' said Mr. Vellam, 'is to obtain probate of Uncle Neb's earlier, and only genuine will, leaving all his estate to you and your children, The nine thousand pounds could not, I am sure, go to anyone more deserving.'

'You ought to have been a detective, Mr. Vellam!' I said as I thanked him for all he had done.

Mr. Vellam laughed quietly. 'When I think of the professional detectives engaged in this case, my dear,' he answered, 'I am very glad that I am not.'

7

The Vicious Circle

This is the story of a man accursed, of one human being in multi-millions who did not get a fair chance. In a word, I am a sort of scapegoat of Nature. I resent it — bitterly, but there is absolutely nothing I can do about it.

My name is Richard Mills. I am dark, five foot eight, and my age is — Well that's part of the story; but for the sake of convenience let's say that I was thirty-two when the horror started. It's odd, you know, how you don't always appreciate the onset of something enormously significant.

I should have guessed that there was something wrong when, from the age of fifteen I often found myself mysteriously a few hours ahead of the right time without knowing how I had done it. I should also have attached suspicion to repeating actions I had done before. But then all of us have felt that we have done such-and-such a thing before — and so like you I didn't think any more about it — Until the impossible happened!

I had just left the office at 6.15 p.m. (I was then clerk to a big firm of lawyers) and in the usual way I took the elevator to the street level and went outside. The October evening was darkening to twilight and the lights of London were on either side of me as usual, climbing into drear muggy sky.

I remember singing to myself as I swung along. Another day over, Betty to meet, and a cheery evening ahead of both of us . . . But I did not keep that appointment because, you see, I walked into something that was at once beyond all sane imagining.

One moment I was streaking for the 'bus stop — then the next I was in the midst of a completely formless grey abyss. It had neither up nor down, light nor dark, form nor outline. I was running on something solid and yet I couldn't see it, and it was just when I was trying to imagine the reason for this sudden fog that I found myself still running down a broad highway I had never seen in my life before!

I slowed to a standstill and I looked about me. The street had altered inexplicably. It was not grey and dirty but highly glazed, as though the road surface was made of polished black glass. The traffic, too, was strangely designed and almost silent. There were no gasoline fumes: I noticed this particularly. In general the buildings were much the same, only shiny on the façades and somewhat taller.

And the lighting! It was still night, but instead of the usual street illumination there were great elliptical globes swinging in mid-air somehow and casting a brilliance below that had no shadows. Everything had the pallid brightness of diffused daylight.

'Anything the matter?' a pleasant voice asked me.

I turned sharply as a passerby paused. Until now I hadn't noticed that the men and women passing up and down the sidewalk were rather odd in their attire

— the women in particular. The absurd hats, the queer translucent look of their clothes, the multi-coloured paints to enhance their features . . . Still women, eternally feminine — but different. And now this stranger. He was tall and young with pleasant eyes and the most amazingly colourful shirt.

'I noticed you hesitating,' he explained, passing a curious but well-mannered eye over my attire. 'Can I help you?'

It surprised me to find anybody so courteous.

'I'm just wondering — where I am,' I replied haltingly. 'This *is* London, isn't it?

'Yes, indeed.'

'Bond Street?

His look of surprise deepened. 'Why, no,' he said. 'You're on Twenty Seven Street. Don't you remember that all street names were abolished ten years ago to avoid duplication?'

I could only gaze at him fixedly, and he gave a slight smile.

'Look here, you're mixed up somewhere,' he said, taking my arm. 'It's part of the city's 'Lend-a-Hand' policy for us

194

to help each other, so I'm going to make you my especial charge . . . Incidentally, the 'Lend-a-Hand' policy is a good idea, don't you think?' he asked, forcing me to stroll along with him. 'It's done away with a lot of the old backbiting.'

'Oh, surely,' I agreed, weakly. 'But look here — Er — what sort of cars are those? They're very quiet.'

'You mean the atom-cars? Say, where *have* you lived? And if you'll forgive me, that's an awfully old-fashioned coat you've got on. I know it's a breach of courtesy, but . . . '

I dragged to a stop and faced him directly. 'You won't credit this,' I said, 'but only what seems about ten minutes ago I was running down Bond Street, for an ordinary gasoline-driven 'bus. Then I ran into a fog, or something and — suddenly I was here!'

'It would be ill-mannered for me to disbelieve,' he said slowly, regarding me, 'but I *am* puzzled. It may help you if I explain that you are in London — which was resurfaced with plastic in 2030. The present date is October the twelfth, 2038.'

2038. Twenty-five years! Great God!

Somehow I had slipped a quarter of a century ahead of my own time of 2013. You can think of such things but you dare not believe them. Yet, damnit, it had happened! And —

But I had no opportunity to ask my genial friend anything more for he was graying in the return of the mist and I was back again in that blank world where nothing is, or ever was, that is outside time, space, and understanding. I stood wondering and fearful, waiting. This time I sensed that the interval was longer ... but when the mist evaporated it revealed that I was back again in familiar Bond Street, only I had moved some two hundred yards from the 'bus stop — or in other words the precise distance I had walked with the stranger!

I blinked, mopped my perspiring face, then glanced up at a nearby clock. It was 6.20, the exact time when I had started to run for the 'bus. I had left the office at 6.15 — five minutes to get down the street ... Then had my other adventure taken up no time whatever?

With an effort I pulled myself together as I saw one or two passersby looking at me curiously. I had to think this one out — maybe talk it over with Betty Hargreaves since I apparently still had time to meet her.

But she never arrived to keep the appointment. Finally I rang up her apartment, and it was only after the storm with her had subsided that I realized I had arrived back in the same place on the *following evening* — twenty-four hours later!

I smoothed things over with her as best I could, said I had been sent out of town on urgent business, and we promised to meet at the same time and place the following evening. I didn't add 'I hope!' even if I felt like it.

Troubled, I began a contemplative wandering through the city, heading in the general direction of my rented apartment — Just the same I never reached it. To my alarm I once more found myself sailing into greyness, and there was nothing I could do to avoid it. My last vision was of a distant lighted clock pointing to 11.15; then it was gone and I was helpless, baffled, frightened.

In this grey enigma all sense of direction, time, and space vanished. I found it safest to stand still and wait until it cleared. It did so eventually and I discovered I was lying in bed in a quiet little room with a grey oblong of window revealing the night sky. I stirred restlessly, puzzled, and reached out a hand for the bedside lamp. When I scrambled out of bed and looked down at myself I got an even bigger shock.

I had the figure of a boy of seven years! I was just as I *had* looked at seven! With a kind of automatic instinct I went to the dressing table and stared at myself in the mirror. There was no doubt about it. I was a child once more, in my own little bedroom at home in Manchester. My parents must be asleep in the next room, but somehow I didn't dare go and look . . . Yet I had the memory of everything I had done up to the age of thirty-two!

Impossible! Idiotic! I had grown backwards!

Returning to the bed I threw myself

upon it and struggled to sort the puzzle out. But gradually that impalpable mist came creeping back and I left the world of my childhood, wandered for a while in blank unknown, and then merged back into the street from which I had disappeared.

The first thing I saw was that lighted clock ahead. It was still at 11.15. Presumably I had once again been absent exactly twenty-four hours — and I had travelled twenty-five years backwards, even as on the other occasion I had travelled twenty-five years forwards.

Can you wonder that I was sick at heart, perplexed? It appeared then that my intervals in 'normal' time last lasted about five hours — or to be exact 4 hours 55 minutes. Queer how I cold bloodedly weighed this up. I felt like a visitor who has only five hours to stay in a town before going on his way.

When presently I encountered a police officer I asked him what day it was, and his rather suspicious answer confirmed my theory of a twenty-four hour absence. I got away from him before he ran me in and went straight to Betty Hargreaves' apartment. Fortunately she had not yet gone to bed, and she eyed me with chilly disfavour when we were in the lounge.

'I suppose I cooled my heels because you had urgent business again?' she asked, going over to the sideboard and mixing me a drink. 'I've got a telephone, you know. You could have *told* me!'

'I'm sorry about that appointment, Bet. I just couldn't keep it. I — er — ' I hesitated over the right phrasing. 'I sort of keep coming and going.'

'You're telling me?'

She handed me my drink and raised a finely lined eyebrow. Betty is a pretty girl, a slim blonde with eyes that are really blue and hair that is really golden. But when she looks annoyed — Whew!

'I never heard of a financier's chief clerk coming and going as much as you do,' she commented presently, sitting down on the divan beside me. 'What's happening, Dick? Is there a merger on, or what?'

'No. It's — er — ' I put the drink down and caught at her arm. 'Bet, I need help!

I'm in one hell of a spot.'

'Money, or a girl?' she questioned dryly. 'If the former I can help you out. Dad didn't exactly leave me penniless. If the latter then let's say good night and thanks for the memory.'

'Nunno — it's neither,' I said. 'It's so hard to explain . . . You see, I — I keep seeing the future and the past!'

Be it said to her everlasting credit that she did not even blink. She just gazed, as one might at lunatic, a baby, or a dipsomaniac. And while she gazed I talked, the words tumbling over themselves. I told her everything, and when I had finished I expected her to laugh in my face. Only she didn't. Instead she was thoughtful.

'It's mighty odd,' she said seriously. 'And because I know you haven't a scrap of imagination and are too gosh-darned honest to lie for no reason I believe you. But — it's crazy!' She hugged herself momentarily. 'And what are we going to, do about it?'

'We!' Bless the girl! She was on my side.

'I dunno,' I muttered. 'As far as I can estimate I am allowed five hours to live like an ordinary man — then off I go! I don't know if a doctor could explain it, or maybe a psychiatrist.'

'Hardly a doctor, Dick.' She shook her fair head musingly. 'It isn't as though you've got a pain. It's more like an illusion. You might do worse than see Dr. Pembroke. He's a psychiatrist in the Aldwych Trust Building. I know because a cousin of mine went to him for treatment.'

I made up my mind. 'I'll see him at the first opportunity. It won't be in the morning because I expect I'll be veered off again at about four fifteen in the small hours. When I can catch up on normal working hours I'll see what he can do for me.'

For ridiculous conversation this probably hit an all time high, yet so sure was I of the things that had happened to me and so staunch was Betty's loyalty, we might have been talking of the next football match. Anyway she was a great comfort to me, and when I left her around 12.30 it was with the resolve to master my trouble when it came upon me again.

I went home to my rooms, learned from a note under the door that my firm had telephoned to inquire what had happened to me — and then I went to bed! Funny, but I wasn't tired in spite of everything, and I must have gone to sleep quite normally; but when I awoke again I was not in my bedroom though I was in pyjamas.

It took me several minutes to get the hang of an entirely new situation. I was lying on my back on closely cropped and very green grass. The air was chilly but not unpleasantly so, and the sky overhead was misty blue with the sun just rising. I judged it was still October, but extremely mild.

As I stood up I got a shock. A small group of men and women — attired so identically it was only by their figures I could tell any difference in sex — was watching me. Embarrassed, I stared back at them across a few yards of soft grass, then I was astonished to behold the foremost man and woman suddenly float over to me with arms outstretched on either side. They settled beside me and silver-coloured wings folded back flat on their backs.

'I know,' I sighed, as they appraised me. 'I've no right to be here and I'm in the future. All right, lock me up: It won't make any difference.'

The man and woman exchanged glances and I had the time to notice that they were both remarkable specimens — tall, strong, athletic-looking, with queer motors strapped to their waist belts from which led wires to the wings on their backs.

After a good deal of cross-talk I found out that they belonged to the local police force, made up of an equal number of men and women, and that I was, of course, both a trespasser and an amazing specimen to boot . . . But this time, it appeared, I had slipped ahead not twenty-five years but *two hundred!*

I suppose, were I a literary man, I could fill a book with the marvels I discovered, but here it is only policy to sketch in the principal advancements. I learned that their amazing system of individual flight had led to the abolition of ordinary aircraft; that they had conquered space, mastered telepathy, overcome the vagaries of the climate, and completely outlawed war. Yes, it was a fair and prosperous land I saw in 2213.

In the end they locked me up for examination by their scientists, but of course it did them no good, for as time passed I faded away from the prison cell and was back again in London, still in my pyjamas, in the middle of a street — and (I soon discovered) at 4.15 in the morning! Once again, twenty-four hours — since presumably I had vanished while asleep at 4.15 twenty-four hours before.

To be thus thinly clad on an October early morning is no picnic. I took the one sensible course and presented myself at a police station, told the sergeant in charge that I had been sleepwalking and had just awakened. I was believed and I got shelter and a borrowed suit of clothes in which to creep home to my rooms in the early dawn hours.

Now I was getting really frightened! If this were to go on — Lord! I did some computing and figured that I had until about 9.15 in the morning before I'd take another trip — so before that time I had got to see Dr. Pembroke. Unlikely that he would be at his office so early unless the urgency of the reason were stressed.

I rang up Betty, told her what had occurred, and asked her advice. She suggested that I tell Pembroke over the 'phone at his home what had happened, and try to get him to be at his office before nine. She promised to be there.

Dr. Pembroke did not sound at all enthusiastic at first, but he warmed up a trifle when I went into explicit details. Finally he seemed interested enough to agree to be at his consulting rooms by 8.45. So it was arranged, and promptly at quarter to nine I was there with Betty, very serious and determined, beside me.

Grant Pembroke was up to time — a tall, eagle-nosed man with very sharp grey eyes and a tautly professional manner. He ushered us both into his consulting room with its rather overpowering looking apparatus, and then switched on softly shaded lights and motioned me to be seated in their immediate focus while Betty sat in the margin of the shadows.

'So, Mr. Mills, you keep imagining you float away into the future and the past at regular intervals, eh?' he asked slowly, settling down and fixing me with those piercing eyes.

'I don't imagine it, Doc — it actually happens,' I told him. 'And in about fifteen minutes it should happen again, then you'll see for yourself.'

'Mmmm.' He made a brief examination of me as though he were a medical man, then sat back in his chair again and put his fingertips together. 'And while you are away twenty-four hours elapse here?' he questioned thoughtfully.

'That's correct, yes.'

'Do twenty-four hours elapse in the place you — er — visit?'

'No. It varies a lot . . . Only definite timing I've noticed is that on the last occasion I leapt two hundred years ahead instead of the former twenty five.'

'Just so, just so . . . A most interesting

sidelight on Time.'

'I don't want to be an interesting sidelight!' I protested fiercely. 'I want to live like any other man, marry the girl I love, and keep my job. As things are I look like losing the lot . . . This sort of thing is — unthinkable!'

'Mmm, just so,' he agreed. 'But there is the other side, you know — We are dealing with a paradox of Time that has so far only been a theory and never proven. You may have the good fortune to be that living proof!'

I could only assume that he had queer ideas on what constitutes good fortune; and so I kept quiet. For another long minute he studied me, then turning to his desk he began to scribble something down on a notepad. He also made calculations and a drawing that looked like a plus sign with a circle running through it I was just about to ask him the purpose of this doodling when things happened — once again.

Even as I felt myself drifting into grey mist I noticed the electric clock stood at exactly 9.15; that Betty and Pembroke had jumped to their feet in stunned amazement — Then off I went. And this movement was backwards in Time, not forward.

When the mists cleared I was seated on a wagon, driving a horse leisurely along a winding country road. I saw I was wearing rough breeches and a flannel shirt, while a hot sun was blazing down on my battered straw hat. A yokel? A farmer? A pioneer? I had never been any of these things as far as I could remember — yet here it was.

Glancing inside the wagon I saw a woman and a boy and girl asleep — and far behind my wagon were many more of similar design kicking up a haze of dust across the desert.

I had to work discreetly to find out what was going on, and very astonished I was to discover that my name was Joseph Kendal, and that the three in the wagon were my wife and two children. We were heading for Georgia, and this — according to my wife — was 1813. We were changing our domicile, every one of us . . . But all that signified to me was that I had dropped back two hundred years even as before I had gone ahead for a similar period.

I scarcely remember what happened while I was there. It seemed to be an endless trip across the desert with all the old pioneering flavour about it. I fitted into it without any effort: everything I did seemed reasonable and natural, and secretly I was rather sorry when it all had to come to an end just after sunset and I was in the grey mists of Between, Beyond, or whatever it is.

I returned to normalcy seated in that same chair in Dr. Pembroke's consulting room. He was opposite me, looking very weary and untidy. Betty, who had apparently been half-asleep in the chair on the rim of the shadows jerked into life as I sat gazing at her. I glanced round and noticed two white-coated nurses and two men who looked like scientists — My eyes moved to the clock. 9.15, and judging from the window it was daylight.

'Twenty-four hours to the minute!' Pembroke exclaimed, getting up and coming over to me. 'Upon my soul, young man, you didn't exaggerate — We've been waiting; and waiting, ever since you disappeared from view. I summoned the nurses in case of need, and these two gentlemen here are scientists with whom I've been discussing your problem.'

'The point is: have you got the answer?' I asked irritably.

'Yes. Yes, indeed,' Pembroke assented, and the two scientists nodded their heads in grave confirmation. 'But,' he added, 'it is rather a grim answer . . . '

'I don't mind that,' I said. 'Can I be *cured*?'

They were silent. I set my jaw and glanced helplessly at Betty. She could only stare back at me, tired from the long vigil, and I thought I saw tears in her eyes as though she were trying to control an inner grief. At last I looked back at Pembroke.

'Tell me what you have done and where you have been,' he instructed.

I did so, and finished bitterly, 'Well, let's have it! What *is* wrong with me?'

He hesitated, then going over to his desk he handed me a sheet of paper on which was a curious looking drawing, the finished effort that I had seen him commence just before I had evaporated. The drawing looked like a plus sign. The horizontal line was marked 'Past' at the left hand end, and 'Future' at the right hand end. Where the vertical line intercepted it in the centre was the word 'Now.' This same 'Now' was also inscribed at top and bottom of the vertical line. So far, so good. Now came the odd bit — starting from the exact centre of the plus sign was an ever widening curve, just like the jam line inside a Swiss roll. You know how that line circles out wider and wider! Well, that is what it looked like, and of course it inevitably crossed the right hand section of the horizontal line marked 'Future', and the left hand line marked 'Past'.

So I sat staring at this drawing that looked as though it had come out of 'Alice in Wonderland' then Pembroke started speaking.

'Young man, I don't want to be blunt, but I have to. You are a freak of Nature! Every human being, every animal, every *thing* is following a Time Line through space, and that line is *straight*. You may recall Sir James Jeans' observations on this in his 'Mysterious Universe'?'

I shook my head. 'I never read Jeans.'

'Mmm, too bad. Then let me quote the relevant statement on page one forty two of my copy . . . ' Pembroke picked up an ancient blue-covered paperback. 'He says — 'Your body moves along the Time Line like a bicycle wheel, and because of this your consciousness touches the world only at one place at one time, just as only part of the cycle wheel touches the road at one time. It may be that Time is spread out in a straight line, but we only contact one instant of it as we progress from past to future . . . In fact, as Weyl has said — 'Events do not happen: we merely come across them.'' End quote . . . '

'And what has this to do with me?' I demanded.

'Just this.' Pembroke returned the book to his desk. '*Your* Time Line is not *straight*. It operates in a circle, like that circular design you see there. You told me that in earlier life you noticed you were unaccountably late sometimes and unusually early at others?'

'Ye — es,' I agreed, thinking. 'That's right enough.'

'That,' Pembroke mused, 'can be taken as evidence of the first aberrations in the Time Line you were following. Now it has taken its first real curve. Instead of progressing normally in a straight line you are carried into hyperspace — that grey mist you have mentioned — which is non-dimensional, non-solid: in a word, plain vacuum — '

'But I lived and breathed!' I interrupted.

'Are you *sure*?' he asked quietly.

I hesitated. Now I came to think back, I wasn't!

'You can no more be sure you lived and breathed than you can be sure of what you do under anaesthetic,' he said. 'But you were still heading along a Time Line — not of your own volition, mind you, but inevitably, because Time sweeps along with it. And so, when the curve struck the normal straight Time Line leading from past to future — the *world* Line, that is, which Earth herself is following — you

214

became a part of it again, but you were twenty-five years ahead of the present.'

I nodded slowly. So far he made sense.

'You stayed there for a period of which you are uncertain, chiefly because your sense of Time had become catastrophically upset; and then, still impelled along this circular Time Line you came back through hyperspace and once more intersected the normal Now Line exactly twenty-four hours afterwards. Events then proceeded normally for a while -- *still* following the circle — you passed through hyperspace to a past event. Then, hyperspace once more, and so back to Now.'

'Then — as the circles grow larger from the centre the gaps will become correspondingly greater?' I questioned, and my voice sounded as though it did not belong to me.

'Just so; and the mathematical accuracy of first twenty-five and then two hundred years — forward and backward — shows that the problem is not a disorder but a mathematical fluke quite beyond human power to alter. You move in a circle, Mr.

Mills, not a straight line, and unless at some point the circle turns back on itself — an unlikely possibility since the Universe is a perfect cyclic scheme — I can foresee nothing else but . . . endless circular travelling, gradually taking in vast segments of Time until . . . '

Pembroke stopped and the room seemed deathly quiet. For some reason though, I was calm now the thing was explained. 'Can you account for my not feeling tired?' I asked presently.

'Certainly. You somewhat resemble a battery. You use up energy in a forward movement into Time because you are, in essence, moving into the unexplored — but in the backward movement the energy replaces itself because you are merely returning to a state already lived. You cannot grow old, or tired, or suffer from ketabolism in the ordinary way because you represent a perfect balance between ketabolism and anabolism, the exact amount of each being equal because each journey is the same amount of Time — namely, first twenty-five, then two hundred. And next — Well, who knows?'

'Look here,' I said slowly. 'This last time I went back two hundred years, as I told you, but I was somebody else! A pioneer or something of two centuries ago. I was never *that*!'

'In a past life you must have been,' he answered calmly. 'Otherwise you could not have taken over that identity.'

'Then when I *was* that person why didn't I know what lay in the future?'

'Perhaps you did. Can you be sure that you didn't?'

This was becoming involved all right, but after all . . . No, damnit, I couldn't answer it. Maybe I *had* known!

'And when I was a boy of seven?' I asked. 'I presume I became a boy again because I was just that at that age?'

'Just so. Time-instants are indestructible. You are bound to become at a certain instant what you are *at* that instant, otherwise Time itself would become a misnomer. You will ask why, at seven years of age, you did not know what you would do at thirty-two . . . ? Again I say, are you sure you didn't?'

'I — I don't know. I don't think so

— unless it was buried in my subconscious or something.'

'It must have been. It was there, that knowledge, but maybe you considered it as just a dream fancy and thought no more about it, just as we speculate on how we may look in, say, ten years time and then dismiss it as pure imagination. But with you such an imagining would be fact. And incidentally, as for your carrying a memory of these present experiences about with you, remember that your physical self is all that is affected by Time. Mind and memory cannot alter.'

'And — what happens now?' I simply dragged the words out.

'For your sake, young man, I hope things will straighten out for you — but if they don't I have a proposition . . . Tell me, have you any relatives?'

'None living, no. I was intending to marry Miss Hargreaves here very soon.'

'Mmmrn, just so. Well, the Institute of Science is prepared to subsidize a Trust by which anybody you may name can benefit. In return we ask that in your swing back to the Now Line you will give

218

us every detail of what has been happening to you during your absences . . . '

I shook my head bewilderedly. 'I'll — I'll do it willingly, but *I* don't want the money. And Bet — Miss Hargreaves, has plenty of money anyway . . . Doc, isn't there some way?' I asked desperately. 'I can tell from you making this proposition that you . . . '

'I'm sorry, Mr. Mills; I really am. But no human agency can get to grips with your problem.'

I was silent through a long interval, Betty seated now at my side. I looked at her, hopelessly.

'Bet, sweetheart, what do *you* say? Do you know anybody who needs money in trust?'

'No!' she answered bitterly. 'Money is the cheapest, most earthly compensation science can offer you for a ruined life. I don't want any part of it . . . Oh, Dick, for God's sake, there must be some way out of this!'

I shook my head. There wasn't. I knew it now . . . Finally I told Pembroke that the money had better be handed over to scientific research, and on my all too infrequent returns to Now I would tell all I knew.

'We could marry,' I whispered to Betty. 'Only it wouldn't be fair to you. A day might come when I'll never return.'

'It will,' Pembroke confirmed quietly. 'When your circular line takes so wide an orbit that it passes beyond the ends of the Now Line into hyperspace.'

Then I was doomed indeed! All I could hope for was an occasional glimpse of Betty. As for the rest . . .

My five-hour stay was taken up in signing legal documents; then once more I was swept inevitably into hyperspace. So I went through that grey enigma which baffles description, and this time I was six hundred years ahead of the Now Line. There was still progress, the building of superb cities, the conquest of other worlds, a sense of greater equality and comradeship between both sexes . . .

So back to Now for a brief spell with a tearful Betty, a long description of my experiences to the scientists, a banquet in my honour at the Science Institute

— then outwards and backwards into the past, for a gap of another six hundred years.

Back and forth as the circle widened.

I have tried to keep out of this narrative the inner horror I experienced at it all — the dull, dead futility of being flung by nameless force into an ever-widening gulf. Each time, of course, as the circle widened I went further afield.

Hundreds of years, thousands of years, from one end of the pendulum's swing to the other — backwards into scores of lives which had long since been effaced from memory; forwards into a wonder world of ever increasing splendour . . . Then in the tens of thousands of years ahead I saw Man was pretty close to leaving his material form altogether and becoming purely mental. So much so that on my visit after this one Earth was empty and turning one face to the sun. Age, old and remorseless, crawled over a once busy planet.

At the opposite end of the scale life was swinging down into the Neanderthal man stage, and then further back still to where

Man was not even present. But there were amoeba, the first forms of life, and I fancy I must have been one of these!

Backwards — forwards — with the visions of Now mere shadows in a universe which was to me insane. Nothing held sense any more. I was losing touch with every well remembered thing, with the dear girl who always awaited my comings and goings — growing older, but always loyal. And around her the cold, impersonal scientists logging down information that could chart the course of civilizations for ages to come. No wonder I had seen progress ahead! My own guidance had prevented any mistakes, and in those distant visions I had seen the fruit of my own advice! Incredible — yet true.

Gradually I realized that my Time Circle was now becoming so huge that it was involving a stupendous orbit that did not include Earth but the Universe as a whole, proving how independent of normal Time Lines had my vicious circle become.

In my swing I saw the birth of the

Earth and the gradual slowing down of the Universe — and this I think is destined to be my last return to the Now Line, for the next curve will be so enormous that — Well, I do not think I shall be able to contact the Now Line at all. The scientists have charted it all out for me.

The curve will take me to the period of the initial explosion that created the expanding universe out of — what? That will be in the past. And my futureward movement will carry me to that state of sublime peace where all the possible interchanges of energy have been made, where there exists thermodynamic equilibrium and the death of all that is. At either end of the curve Time is *non-existent!* This is where I may at last find rest.

As I think on these things, writing these last words in the world of Now, I cannot help but marvel at what I have done . . . But I hate it! I hate it with all my human soul! Opposite to me in this bright room Betty is seated, silent, dry-eyed, faithful to the last. Science is still represented in the quiet men in the chairs by the far wall, all of them busy writing and checking notes.

Never was so strange a sentence passed on a human being!

The greyness is coming! I have no time to write any more —

THE END

CLIMATE INCORPORATED
THE FIVE MATCHBOXES
EXCEPT FOR ONE THING
BLACK MARIA, M.A.
ONE STEP TOO FAR
THE THIRTY-FIRST OF JUNE
THE FROZEN LIMIT
ONE REMAINED SEATED
THE MURDERED SCHOOLGIRL
SECRET OF THE RING
OTHER EYES WATCHING
I SPY . . .
FOOL'S PARADISE
DON'T TOUCH ME
THE FOURTH DOOR
THE SPIKED BOY
THE SLITHERERS
MAN OF TWO WORLDS
THE ATLANTIC TUNNEL
THE EMPTY COFFINS
LIQUID DEATH
PATTERN OF MURDER
NEBULA
THE LIE DESTROYER
PRISONER OF TIME

MIRACLE MAN
THE MULTI-MAN
THE RED INSECTS
THE GOLD OF AKADA
RETURN TO AKADA
GLIMPSE
ENDLESS DAY
THE G-BOMB
A THING OF THE PAST
THE BLACK TERROR
THE SILENT WORLD
DEATH ASKS THE QUESTION
A CASE FOR BRUTUS LLOYD
LONELY ROAD MURDER
THE HAUNTED GALLERY
SPIDER MORGAN'S SECRET
BURY THE HATCHET
EXPERIMENT IN MURDER
MOTIVE FOR MURDER

We do hope that you have enjoyed reading this large print book.

Did you know that all of our titles are available for purchase?

We publish a wide range of high quality large print books including:
Romances, Mysteries, Classics
General Fiction
Non Fiction and Westerns

Special interest titles available in large print are:
The Little Oxford Dictionary
Music Book, Song Book
Hymn Book, Service Book

Also available from us courtesy of Oxford University Press:
Young Readers' Dictionary
(large print edition)
Young Readers' Thesaurus
(large print edition)

For further information or a free brochure, please contact us at:
Ulverscroft Large Print Books Ltd.,
The Green, Bradgate Road, Anstey,
Leicester, LE7 7FU, England.
Tel: (00 44) **0116 236 4325**
Fax: (00 44) **0116 234 0205**

RENEGADE LEGIONNAIRE

Gordon Landsborough

General Sturmer, formerly a Nazi officer in the German desert forces, now leads a group of renegade Arab headhunters, tracking down Foreign Legion deserters — a lucrative business. Meanwhile, ex-cowboy Legionnaire Texas is planning revenge. He aims to capture Sturmer and bring him to face justice in America for his war crimes. In Tunisia, during the war, Sturmer had been responsible for the deaths of thousands of prisoners . . . and one of them had been Tex's brother . . .

DEVIL'S PLAGUE

Michael R. Collings

On a summer's morning, a young woman's body lay battered and broken at the bottom of Porcupine Falls. Who was responsible? Was it the local boy, who was so enamoured with her? Or the stranger with the hidden past? And what is the role of the Devil's Plague? It is up to Lynn Hanson and her friend, Victoria Sears, to examine the clues left by the killer and explain the mystery of the death at Porcupine Falls.

CASEY CLUNES INVESTIGATES

Geraldine Ryan

A pregnant Casey Clunes investigates a case of baby snatching. Young Gemma Stebbings' baby has disappeared from the nursery at Brockhaven Hospital. But all the CCTV footage of medical staff and visitors reveals nothing — so where is baby Justin, and who is responsible? *In at the Deep End* finds Casey attending a reception for a Cambridge college's new swimming pool at Doughty Hall. Author Susannah Storey performs the opening ceremony . . . then her dead body is discovered, floating in the pool . . .

THE CRIMSON RAMBLERS

Gerald Verner

Ready to perform in Andy McKay's concert party on the pier pavilion at Westpool, *The Crimson Ramblers* face more than they imagine . . . As they travel by train to Westpool and enter a dark tunnel, a mysterious packet is thrown into their compartment. Then their summer show becomes a focal point for murder, mystery and sudden death. There are many people anxious to get possession of the packet — who are they? And why are ready to commit murder for it?

SNAKE EYES

Richard Hoyt

John Denson, the Seattle private eye with his partner, Willie Prettybird — a shaman of the Cowlitz tribe — face their deadliest case: an engineered out-break of anthrax in the Pacific Northwest. A ballooning list of suspects includes a rodeo cowboy; a barkeep with a roving eye; an ancient teacher at a high-school reunion — and the chief of police. Then there's the fund-raising televan-gelist Hamm Bonnerton. One of them is playing liar's dice, and coming up snake eyes. And killing people . . .

TERROR LOVE

Norman Lazenby

Married to Gilbert Brand, Kathryn imagines her marriage to be a happy one. It's studded with the parties of her husband's rich, socialite friends. But their attendance at a party given by his business associate, Victor Milo, tarnishes Brand's suave image. Kathryn discovers Brand attempting to strangle another guest, the nightclub singer Claudia, who becomes Kathryn's bitterest enemy. Then her world begins to crumble as she learns that Brand is an unscrupulous criminal . . . and she begins a descent into terror.